T0367903

## ALSO BY KAY SALTER

Twelfth Summer

Thirteenth Summer

Fourteenth Summer

Fifteenth Summer

Sixteenth Summer

**To order copies please contact** jsalter8@hotmail.com

# Seventeenth Summer

## The Sarah Bowers Series

## Kay Salter

authorHOUSE®

*AuthorHouse*™
*1663 Liberty Drive*
*Bloomington, IN 47403*
*www.authorhouse.com*
*Phone: 1-800-839-8640*

© *2012 by Kay Salter. All rights reserved.*

*No part of this book may be reproduced, stored in a retrieval system, or transmitted by any means without the written permission of the author.*

*Published by AuthorHouse    03/22/2012*

*ISBN: 978-1-4685-6045-9 (sc)*
*ISBN: 978-1-4685-6046-6 (hc)*
*ISBN: 978-1-4685-6047-3 (e)*

*Library of Congress Control Number: 2012904301*

*Any people depicted in stock imagery provided by Thinkstock are models, and such images are being used for illustrative purposes only.*
*Certain stock imagery © Thinkstock.*

*This book is printed on acid-free paper.*

*Because of the dynamic nature of the Internet, any web addresses or links contained in this book may have changed since publication and may no longer be valid. The views expressed in this work are solely those of the author and do not necessarily reflect the views of the publisher, and the publisher hereby disclaims any responsibility for them.*

# Gratitudes

My friend Mary Beth Correll has seen me through what is now the sixth book in the Sarah Bowers series. She patiently tames and pats into place my runaway thoughts much as one forms cookie dough into pleasing shapes before the oven. Bless her heart.

I am indebted to Amy and Dot for patiently policing grammar, punctuation and capitalization. It's a tough job but someone has to do it. Thankfully, not me.

Gratitude and thankfulness go to God for giving us Sarah, the girl on the cover of the book and the light and love of my life.

# Dear Santa . . .

I was thrilled to learn recently that Fifteenth Summer was on a Christmas list for the year 2011. The young hopeful was a girl nine years old who lives in Seattle, Washington.

The same year a friend and former teacher placed Fifteenth Summer on her Christmas list. She was ninety-three years old and lives in Marshallberg, North Carolina.

My thanks and gratitude to these ladies and all the readers in between.

Kay Salter

# Contents

# Chapter 1

"Oh, Lindsay, I can't come to Rachel's end of year party! We're leaving on vacation." Sarah Bowers, daughter of Peggy and James Bowers was on the telephone with her best friend, Lindsay Piner.

"Can't you wait one more day? What is so important in that little town that one more day would make a bit of difference?"

Sarah lay sprawled across the sofa, the heavy, black receiver jammed against one ear. She waved a foot in the air, admiring her new white, summer sandals. "Now, Lindsay . . ." she was suddenly interrupted by her friend's loud voice in the receiver.

"Come in this house now, Allison. Mama didn't say you could go to Callie's while she's gone."

Sarah could hear Lindsay's younger sister protesting loudly in the background. "I can't go with you, Allison. I'm watching Alex while mama buys groceries."

Allison's wail of protest was easily heard. "Honestly, Lindsay, you would think that since we are high school seniors, our younger brothers and sisters would show us a little respect."

Lindsay sighed. "I can endure everything except being included in my father's lectures about proper behavior. Sometimes he makes me feel like I'm still a little kid."

"Right! How do you think I feel when mama or daddy start a sentence with, 'Now children,' and there I stand, a head taller than mama."

"I have to go, Sarah. It sounds like Allison is teasing Alex, or vice versa. Have a wonderful summer, and write if you meet any cute boys."

Sarah continued lying on the sofa, the heavy black phone perched on her stomach. While the house was fairly quiet, she knew this was a good chance to say farewell to each of her friends.

Before she could finish her list, Peggy Bowers came in the room carrying the day's mail.

"Sarah, you have a letter."

Surprised, Sarah quickly sat up, and put the telephone on the table. "Who's it from, Mama?"

Peggy Bowers, studying the envelope, shook her blonde curls and grinned at her older daughter. "I believe it's from your friend in Beaufort, Nancy Russert."

"Why would she go to the trouble to write, when she knows we'll soon be there? It must be something very important." She sat up straight, turning the pale pink envelope over in her hand. Anxious, she tore it open. Inside was stationary, the same pale pink color. Delicate vines with pink roses graced the margins of each sheet. The handwriting, every letter formed perfectly, made Sarah smile. Nancy Russert, her summer pal in Beaufort, was a model of perfection in her starched clothes, precise speech and good manners, always good manners. Her dedication to practicing piano left Sarah bewildered. Nancy's dream was to someday be a concert pianist with the North Carolina Symphony, and she worked toward this goal with diligence and determination. "I know I'm no prodigy," she'd say, "but I'll make up for it with hard work." Sarah admired and even envied Nancy, since she wasn't sure what she wanted to be when she finished school.

Sarah drew her legs up and leaned against the soft sofa cushions covered in splashes of flowered fabric. Spooky, Sarah's cat, needed no invitation to climb in the girl's lap and begin purring.

*Dear Sarah,*

*I sincerely hope this letter finds you and your family in good health. My parents enjoyed a winter free of illness. I, however, suffered nine days with a chest cold. I had to stay home from school and rest in bed. I didn't feel like practicing piano for six days.*

Sarah grinned and looked at her sleepy pet. "Spooky, your Aunt Nancy never changes. She is as precise as ever. Now, I would have said I was sick for two weeks and be done with it." Sarah whispered, "It's the only rest her piano will ever get." Sarah was rewarded with a loving glance through her pet's half closed eyes.

*I am writing to tell you of an event which is coming soon. The music teacher at Beaufort High is directing a concert of songs popular during World Wars I and II. The theme is celebrating peace. Guess who she asked to accompany the chorus? Me! I am so thrilled. It will be my first concert appearance!*

*Now, Sarah, there will be try-outs every night this week. I know you have a beautiful voice, because I've sat beside you in junior choir at St. Paul's every Sunday for many summers. Wouldn't it be something if you landed a solo part, and I played for you? That would be thrilling!*

*Please call me as soon as you get to Beaufort. We have some exciting things to discuss.*

*Your friend,*
*Nancy Russert*

"Mama," called Sarah, "do you have time to listen to Nancy's letter?"

"Sure. Let me check on Amy. I worry when she's this quiet."

Their mother placed the rest of the mail on the hall table and walked toward the kitchen.

"Amy's fine, Mama. I gave her a coloring book and a box of crayons. That should hold her for a few minutes. I even put down newspaper to protect the table."

"That's good, honey, but I'm not worried about hurting the finish on the top of that old oak table. If your father didn't scar it when he was a boy, and it survived you and Joshua, I'm not worried about crayon wax. So, what does Nancy have to say?" asked Peggy, sitting down in an overstuffed chair. She twirled a blonde curl and listened while her older daughter read the letter. When Sarah finished she looked over at her mother and smiled.

"I think it would be fun to be in a small town production, Mama. I'm sure to get at least one solo part because I've been in productions at Broughton High for three years."

Peggy Bowers rose, preoccupied with the silence in the kitchen. "It sounds like fun, honey. You and Nancy would enjoy going to practice together," she said over her shoulder. Before she could reach the kitchen door, Amy came out, proudly holding a piece of paper.

"Look, Mama, see my picture?" The four year old proudly held the art so her mother could admire it.

"Yes, Amy. That's very colorful."

"Did we get a letter from Granny Jewel today?" asked Sarah.

A troubled look crossed the mother's face. "No, not today," she said slowly, "but, I can tell by her letters she is worried about your Aunt Miriam. I think Mama will be relieved when we get there."

"There's nothing we can do. Aunt Miriam is the one having a baby."

"We can provide moral support."

"Is that like filling in the gap?"

"I'm not sure it's the same thing. Filling in the gap is something our family has always done. If one needs something, or experiences a loss, the rest of us try in some way to make it better."

Sarah smiled, "I remember if I skinned my knee, or lost a baby tooth, there was always something, like a chocolate milk shake, or a new toy, to take my mind off the hurt. A milk shake or a double dip of ice cream isn't enough to make my problems disappear now that I'm older. I depend on God and my family for protection."

"Mama, Mama, look at my picture," demanded Amy.

"Yes, dear, it's very nice. Tell me all about it."

While Amy chirped, Sarah looked about the room she knew she wouldn't see for three months. The walls were painted a soft cream, drapes of flowered chintz graced the windows, softening the Venetian blinds which were closed each night for privacy. A maroon wool rug covered the floor, with only a small margin of hardwood flooring showing around the edge. Tall lamps, with shades of silk, graced the tables on each end of the sofa. Sarah smiled when she thought how she and her brother had been instructed many times to not rough-house in the living room because they might break something. Her thoughts were interrupted by her little sister's strident voice.

"You're not looking, Sarah. Pay attention."

"I'm sorry, Amy. I promise to do better."

"I'm going to make another picture. This one will be for daddy." The four year old scrambled from her mother's lap and returned to the kitchen.

Sarah smiled at her mother. "What do you want, Mama, a niece or a nephew?"

Peggy Bowers smoothed wrinkles from her skirt. "Another boy would be nice. Even though your brother would be eleven years older, Joshua can teach him how to fish and play ball."

"I want the baby to be a girl," declared Sarah. "Girls are fun to dress up and put bows in their hair. And, they're not as *loud*. Boys smell funny when they've been out playing all day."

Amy appeared in the doorway. "A baby doesn't have to be a people. It can just be a baby."

"Ah, out of the mouth of babes," laughed mother. "You are wise, Amy. The baby will be a baby, and we'll be thrilled, no matter if it is a boy or girl."

By two o'clock the following day, the little family crossed the bridge leading into the small sea coast town of Beaufort. Ann Street, shaded by green boughs from towering elms, provided a cool, restful contrast to the blistering heat of the highway. "Hurry, Sarah," came Joshua's voice from the back seat. "I know Papa Tom and Granny Jewel are going to worry until they see us pull up in front of the house."

"I'm driving as fast as I dare, little brother. We wouldn't want to be stopped by the policeman."

Soon, they stopped in front of the graceful Victorian home where Peggy had grown up. On the front porch sat two people. "Oh, my gosh, Mama," said Sarah, glancing at her mother, "Granny Jewel's hair is almost white! I can't believe my eyes!"

Peggy opened the door on the passenger side. "They're getting older, Sarah," she said sadly. "But," she glanced at her older daughter, "Don't say I said it, especially around mama."

"I wouldn't dare," replied Sarah, watching her younger brother and sister being swept into the arms of their waiting grandparents.

Jewel Mitchell met her daughter and older granddaughter with open arms. Sarah folded herself in the familiar embrace. With eyes closed, she inhaled lavender cologne. The faint aroma conjured memories of past summers.

After hugging her daughter, Granny Jewel turned once more to Sarah. Tilting her head, she remarked, "I saw you trying not to look at the color of my hair, Sarah. I'm distressed it has turned gray so suddenly." As they walked slowly up the sidewalk she turned to Peggy "Honey, I'm so worried about Miriam, it's a wonder I have any hair at all."

"What's the matter, Mama," asked Peggy, returning her mother's worried look.

"Your father gets upset if I say anything, but I know he's worried, too." Jewel Mitchell patted her daughter on the shoulder. "We'll have a chance to talk after supper when you're unpacking." She turned to Sarah. "Nancy called this morning and left a message for you to call as soon as you get here."

Sarah stepped on the porch into the waiting arms of her grandfather. "I missed you, Papa Tom." This summer she no longer had to stand on tiptoe to whisper in his ear. It had been her grandfather, summer's past, who taught her how to fish and row a boat. He was a loving, protective grandparent who, by example, had taught his children and grandchildren to do what is morally and ethically right.

"When you went home at the end of last summer, business at the grocery store took a downturn. All the young fellows and eligible bachelors found there was no one to wait on them except three ugly men, so they took their business elsewhere." Sarah, alarmed at first, saw a twinkle in her grandfather's eye and a smile on his lips.

"Papa," she said, shaking a finger at Papa Tom, "I've been here ten minutes, and already you're teasing." Arms entwined, they stepped inside the cool, spacious hall. On the right was a graceful staircase leading to the second floor. In the back of the house, Sarah could hear her brother and sister talking excitedly to Clara, who not only cooked all the meals in the Mitchell house, but held a position of confidante and confessor.

"Bless be! I got my three young'uns back at last after a long, lonesome winter. I can't decide which one of you to hug first." Both younger children clung to her skirt.

While Sarah waited a turn, she looked around the kitchen. For as long as she could remember, the cabinets had been white with red trim, red checked linoleum on the floor. Cheerful white curtains trimmed in red and yellow flowers hung from the windows.

"Clara, is that a pan of homemade rolls rising under that dish towel?" The delicate aroma of yeast bread filled the kitchen.

"I baked a pan for your grandpapa's lunch, and I just happened to put three aside in case we had some hungry folks from out of town drop in." A glass dish with three golden brown rolls sat on the top of the cookstove, covered with wax paper. Clara broke them apart and filled them with wedges of homemade butter from Mrs. Carraway's dairy farm. Three pairs of eyes followed her every move.

"Clara, isn't that a new cook stove?"

"Yes, indeedy! It's brand new, and it's *electric*! No more lighting the oven and almost getting my eyebrows singed."

Sarah bit into the still warm, fluffy roll and felt melted butter ooze between her fingers. The flavor, on her empty stomach, made her eyes roll involuntarily. When the last bite was gone, Sarah turned to Clara. "I'll get my suitcase so I can get unpacked and help you with supper."

"That'll be a blessing, honey. Your aunt and uncle are coming over, and I have a mess of chicken to fry. I'll let you turn it."

"I'd be honored. It's the first summer you've trusted me to help with the cooking."

Clara dried her hands on the hem of her apron and gave Sarah an appraising look. "You're seventeen years old. It's time you learned how to cook and take care of a house. Why, when I was your age, I was keeping house, and cooking for my brand new husband."

Sarah, eyes twinkling, said, "Now, Clara, how can I ever hope to marry? You haven't approved of a single boy I've dated."

"I can't help it if unsuitable suitors follow you home." Clara reached for her long handled, wooden stirring spoon in the dish drainer. Pointing it at Sarah, she declared, "When Mr. Right appears at the door, I'll give him my stamp of approval."

"Suppose he's tall, and has dark red hair."

"Don't you go get worrisome with that kind of talk! Thank the Lord that aggravation is far away in Ohio, and I hope that's where he stays." As Sarah went through the house to get her suitcase, Clara shook her head and mumbled. "But, I got a feeling we haven't seen the last of him."

Sarah, struggling with her suitcase, was in the hall when the telephone rang. "I'll get it," she called.

"Sarah, is that you?" rang Nancy Russert's familiar voice.

"Hi, Nancy. I was going to call you when I got this gigantic suitcase back in my room."

"Do you still occupy the little room behind the kitchen?"

"Yes, that's my hide-away. It may be small but it's all *mine*. No brothers or sisters allowed."

"I have a million things to tell you."

"Me, too."

"Can we meet after supper and go sit on the Inlet Inn dock until bedtime?"

"That sounds great, Nancy. I'm going to help Clara with supper, so Mama will help with the dishes."

"You're lucky to have enough women to do teamwork. Mama and I do it all."

"I'll call you the minute I can get free. Uncle Herb and Aunt Miriam are coming over, so it may take a little longer."

There was silence for a moment. Finally, Nancy spoke. "I saw Mrs. Mitchell a few days ago. Bless her heart! She looked so tired, and so, uh, big. I know she'll be glad when the baby gets here."

"I think we'll all be glad. Nancy, I have to go now. Clara is trusting me to fry the chicken, and I better get in the kitchen."

Sarah hurried to the living room when she heard her relative's voices. She was lifted off her feet in a bear hug by her tall, handsome uncle. "Look, Miriam, it's the world's prettiest grocery clerk." He stopped suddenly and looked serious. "You are going to work this summer, aren't you?"

Sarah sighed. "Oh, yes, if you'll have me. My family believes you can't appreciate a dollar unless you have earned it." Sarah turned to speak to her aunt, her smile fading. Embracing her tenderly, she murmured, "Aunt Miriam, it's so good to see you." Later, Sarah would tell her mother it was difficult to hide her concern behind a smile of greeting. Miriam Mitchell, tall and slender the summer before, was huge, her movements clumsy. Dark circles were under her eyes, her feet and ankles swollen. Sarah glanced at her mother, and saw the same concern mirrored in her face. All were relieved when Clara announced dinner.

"I do think this is the best chicken I ever ate," declared Papa Tom when all were seated and the blessing had been given. "It must have been cooked by tender young hands."

Clara, stepping into the dining room, said, "You've never had any trouble eating your share of fried chicken cooked by these old brown hands."

"You're right," said Papa Tom, winking at Clara. "If you teach Sarah to cook this summer, all the young men will be begging for her hand in marriage."

Clara put hands on her hips and narrowed her eyes. "We already had a little talk about that. This child is much too young to be waiting on some aggravating man. She's got years before she needs to worry about that."

"Clara, you're not hinting I'm aggravating, are you?" asked Papa Tom.

"Humph! You put the 'A' in aggravating. You are the champion aggravator. When you went off to college, you must have studied aggravating, and . . ." "Clara, I think we get the point," laughed Granny Jewel.

Tom Mitchell, looking injured, "Honey, aren't you going to defend me?"

"Phew," sighed Granny Jewel, "I'm afraid there's a lot of truth in what Clara says."

Sarah hurried along the sidewalk. Soft darkness, punctuated by street lights on each corner lit Sarah's way. The cool, night air was welcoming after the heat of the kitchen. As she hurried by, Sarah glanced in windows and saw people moving about, going on with their daily lives. This time of night, families were sitting in their living rooms, listening to programs on the radio. Some had the volume turned so loud she could hear familiar voices from programs her family enjoyed.

She was startled when she heard a man's voice. "Do my eyes deceive me, or is that Jewel and Tom's pretty grand youngun' from Raleigh?"

Sarah paused and laughed. "Hi, Mr. Stewart. You're right, it's me. We got here today, and plan to spend the whole summer."

"Did you and all yours have a good winter?"

Sarah was anxious to move along. However, good manners dictated she stop a minute and visit. "Yes, sir," she answered. "How are Mrs. Stewart and Laney?"

"Mary's getting Laney down for the night, and I'm providing a cafeteria for mosquitoes. I thought it would help if I kept the porch light off, but they found me anyway. Our daughter's growing like a weed, and sharp as a steel tack. That child can do anything she sets her mind to. Why, the other day . . ."

Sarah interrupted, "I'm sorry, Mr. Stewart, but I have to meet Nancy. If I don't hurry, she'll think something awful has happened to me."

Sarah could see Morgan Stewart's smile even in the darkness. "I'll let you go if you promise to stay longer next time."

"I promise, Mr. Stewart." Sarah hurried along the sidewalk, fearful of missing her friend. Soon, from the street light on the corner, Sarah saw the familiar figure of the girl who had been her pal for several summers.

"Yoo hoo, Nancy," Sarah called. Her friend waved in recognition. The soft glow from the corner street light showed Nancy dressed in shorts and matching top. As the girls embraced Sarah noted that her friend had changed very little from the summer before. "You look just the same," said Sarah.

"Do you suppose we've stopped growing at last," laughed Nancy. "I don't have to let the hem out of my skirts any more.

"Your hair is longer."

"I want it to be thick and straight, like yours," answered Nancy wistfully.

"I wish mine were soft and curly, like yours."

They linked arms and walked toward Front Street.

"Oh, well," sighed Nancy

"Yeah, oh well," replied Sarah.

The girls walked to the end of Inlet Inn dock, and kicked off their shoes. Reflected light from nearby stores sent shimmering paths across the dark water. A faint odor of marsh grass and low tide mud wafted across Taylor's Creek. Sarah closed her eyes and inhaled deeply. *This is where I belong, not in the city where exhaust fumes sting your eyes and trucks go thundering by every few minutes.* The lonesome cry of a black skimmer following the shore for a late supper punctuated the silence.

"We're seniors, at last," murmured Nancy. "I thought it would never happen." She kicked the water beneath her bare feet. "Only one more year and I'll be out of this boring town." She turned to her friend. "Some of the girls in my class have quit school and are getting married."

"Married?"

"Sure. Cherry Point Marine Corps Air station is only twenty-five miles away. There are hundreds of lonely marines ready to fall in love."

"It sounds romantic." Sarah poked her friend. "You could marry a marine and live all over the world, Japan, Hawaii, England. Life would be one big adventure." For a minute neither spoke. There was only the sound of gentle waves lapping against the side of a boat moored nearby.

"Think about it, Nancy, you'd never have to do homework again, or get up mornings and go to school. Nobody could tell you what to do. Every night your husband would come home, so handsome in his uniform, sweep you off your feet, and tell you how much he missed you all day."

"That sounds good, Sarah, but suppose you end up in Greenland, a house full of crying babies, and all your diapers frozen to the clothesline? Your husband would come home every night and sweep you off your feet and want to know what's for supper."

"Maybe we'd better stay in school."

"Yes. That sounds like a better plan. Now, Sarah, tryouts for the Fourth of July production start tomorrow night at the high school. Are you in good voice?"

"Yes I am!" answered Sarah, sounding confident.

# Chapter 2

Sarah told Nancy good night at the corner of Ann and Pollock Street. "I have to go home, Nancy. Mama worries when I'm out alone."

Nancy sighed. "I know," she nodded. "My parents are the same way. I can't imagine what evil could befall us in this sleepy town."

When Sarah reached her grandparents' home, she saw her mother and grandmother sitting on the upstairs porch. They waved and smiled. "Come on up," whispered Granny Jewel. "We're talking 'girl talk.'"

Sarah took the tall graceful steps two at a time, being careful not to make a single sound. A chance to be with her mother and grandmother without the clatter and chatter of her younger siblings was a rare treat.

Granny Jewel patted a soft pillow in the bottom of a white wicker chair. Slipping silently into it, she waited expectantly for the conversation to resume.

"Sarah," her mother whispered. "Mama has been telling me of Miriam's ordeal the past few weeks."

"This blistering heat hasn't helped," fretted the grandmother.

"Can't Uncle Herb hire someone to help with the housework?"

"Oh, yes, she has help with the housework four days a week. If Dr. Maxwell orders bed rest for the rest of her time, she'll have to have someone come in every day." Granny Jewel tossed her head, her almost white hair reflected in the glow from the corner street light. "I go over every day or so, but I'm cautious, because she might not want her mother-in-law making suggestions."

"You could go over and help without making suggestions," offered Sarah.

"Wel-l-l, it's not my nature to keep quiet if I know a better way to do things."

"Mother, you can't mean that!" said Peggy trying not to laugh.

"Now my dear daughter, you're teasing me. You should show your mother more respect."

"Yes, Mama." said Peggy, subdued.

Sarah found it fascinating that her grandmother sometimes treated her grown daughter as if she were a wayward child.

"Getting back to Miriam's delicate condition . . ."

Sarah knew her grandmother was once more in charge of the conversation. "Sarah," she said, turning to her granddaughter, "the baby isn't due for another month. Miriam suffers from shortness of breath and her ankles are puffy and swollen. She told me no matter where she sits, she can't get comfortable." Granny Jewel shook her head. "The poor dear had to give up going to church. The pews at St. Paul's are uncomfortable even if you are the picture of health. I won't draw an easy breath until she's sleeping peacefully in the nursery."

"She who?"

"She, meaning the baby, of course," replied Granny Jewel indignantly.

Sarah stared. "How do you know the baby is a girl?"

Granny Jewel gave a loud sniff. "Of course the baby is a girl. I can tell."

Sarah, fascinated by a side of her grandmother she hadn't seen before, leaned forward.

"Well, honey," she replied, "When you have seen as many expectant mothers as I have, you just *know*. Your grandfather is sure and certain the baby is a boy. Men think boy babies are important because they carry on the family name, fight for their country and like to go fishing."

Sarah stared at the faint outline of her mother in the darkness. "Was Daddy disappointed when I was a girl?"

Peggy reached over and took her daughter's hand. "Good Heavens, no! The first time he held you, you clasped your tiny hand around his finger, and around his heart. There is a special bond between a girl and her father."

Granny Jewel stood and stretched. "Girls," she announced, "it's getting late. Tomorrow is a brand new day and we must be rested and ready." With her hand on the screen door, she turned, "This house has come alive once more. I can sense it."

"I feel it, too," whispered Sarah. "It sounds like the house is breathing."

Granny Jewel gave Sarah a hug. "Honey, that's your grandfather snoring. His breathing is more like the roar of a mighty wind."

Sitting down to a breakfast of eggs, bacon, grits, toast and juice, Sarah surveyed her family. Granny Jewel was ordering the day. Papa Tom was teasing Clara and Joshua was eating as rapidly as possible without sacrificing good table manners. Amy, graduated from the highchair, sat on a Sears and Roebuck catalog, her mother patiently helping spear a bite of scrambled egg with a tiny silver fork.

*I've waited for this moment all winter,* she thought. *For three months I can enjoy sleeping late, going to Atlantic Beach, dating* . . . Her grandfather's voice interrupted her thoughts. She glanced at his smiling face. "Excuse me, Papa Tom, what did you say?"

"I asked if you are going to help us at the store this summer." Sarah returned his smile and nodded. *Oh well, I'll add clerking at the grocery store to my list of fun things to do.*

"Mama, may I borrow the car tonight? Nancy and I are going to the high school to try out for the Fourth of July concert. I stand a good chance of getting a solo part, because people tell me I can sing as well as Kate Smith."

"There's a lot of talented people in this town who will be trying out for the lead roles," cautioned Granny Jewel.

"I know, but I have had voice training in Raleigh."

"Are you taking voice lessons?" asked Papa Tom.

"Well, no, but our choir director at church teaches how to sing." Sarah turned to her grandfather. "Do you need me at the store today? I was hoping to finish unpacking and take the kids to the library."

"Not me," answered Joshua quickly. "Mackie and me are going swimming off the government dock."

"Mackie and I," said his mother absently.

Nancy was sitting on her front porch waiting. Sarah noticed she was wearing a flowered dress, white pumps and carried a matching purse. Sarah glanced down. Suddenly she felt dowdy in cotton slacks and a white blouse already damp with perspiration. She wondered fleetingly if Nancy had ever perspired a single drop. "You smell good," she told her friend as she got in the car.

Nancy giggled. "I put a touch of cologne on my wrists and behind each ear. That's how ladies do it in the movies."

"You'll be the sweetest smelling piano player in the whole county."

"I'm the accompanist," answered Nancy, giving a loud sniff.

Sarah grinned. "Well, whatever it's called, you'll be the best."

Several cars were already parked in front of the handsome, red brick school. The girls hurried inside, stopping in the foyer. "I wonder why schools smell the way they do," whispered Sarah, breathing deeply. "Nothing else has that smell, but every school has it."

The girls glanced down the silent corridors, their only illumination the gray twilight seeping through windows above the exits.

"The odor must come from old books, chalk dust and stale air," whispered Nancy.

"How about body emissions? After all, there are at least thirty-five students in every classroom."

"What are you saying Sarah?"

"Oh, Nancy, you know what it's like in class after everyone has eaten a big dinner in the cafeteria."

Nancy closed her eyes and gave a big sniff. "I have no idea what you're talking about."

"A full stomach and sitting still for several hours causes gasses to build in one's tummy. Maybe *that's* why all schools have the same distinctive odor," explained Sarah, grinning.

"Sarah! The very idea! Did you never attend classes on proper subjects for young ladies? There are some things not suitable to mention in polite company."

Sensing her friend's discomfort, Sarah quickly changed the subject. "I hear voices. Maybe the building is haunted."

"They're coming from the auditorium. The auditions are being held in there."

"Ah, Nancy, you're here," called Virginia Hassell, the director. Nancy hurried forward and took her place at the piano. Sarah stood behind a group of people laughing and talking among themselves. *They all know each other,* she observed. In Raleigh there would be a sense of competition among strangers.

"Please have a seat everyone, and we'll go over the songs on the program. We may want to add or drop some of them." When all were seated, she continued. "All the songs will be patriotic, since it is a Fourth of July celebration," announced Mrs. Hassell, her pen poised. Looking up expectantly, she said. "We need a tenor for 'Yankee Doodle Dandy.'" Someone in the second row offered, "Earl Mac would be great." All nodded in agreement.

A bass solo was assigned to Guy Smith, who modestly nodded his assent.

*Where are the other people who want a solo part? Why don't they speak up? These are the strangest auditions I have ever seen,* decided Sarah.

After hurriedly scribbling notes on a stack of crumpled paper, Mrs. Hassell looked up. "The last solo to be assigned is 'God Bless America.'" Her eyes roamed about the expectant faces. "Are there any volunteers?" Several names were mentioned. It seemed as if everyone was talking at once. Fearful of not being given an opportunity to try out, Sarah raised her hand. Suddenly, the director slapped the flat of her hand on the top of the piano. Nancy jumped two inches off the piano bench, her expression never changing. Silence followed.

"Can we help you?" asked Mrs. Hassell, surprised. She looked expectantly toward the girl on the back row. All heads turned, giving Sarah a curious stare.

Sarah replied in a small voice, "I'd like to try out for the solo part." The ceiling of the cavernous room seemed to swallow her voice. Her declaration was met with silence. Finally, the director spoke, "What's your name, honey?"

Sarah cleared her throat. Feeling like a stranger in a strange land, she managed to say, "My name is Sarah Bowers, Ma'am, and I'm visiting relatives." It occurred to Sarah that if she could claim kinship with someone in Beaufort, they wouldn't think she had just arrived from the other side of the world.

"Who are your parents?"

"Peggy and James Bowers, from Raleigh," she added. Her remarks were met with curious stares.

"Who are your grandparents?" asked an older woman.

Sarah shifted her weight and leaned on the back of the chair in front of her. She remembered summers past when the mention of her grandparents' names meant smiles and instant acceptance. "Jewel and Tom Mitchell," she replied in a strong voice. Smiles quickly replaced the curious looks of all present.

"Well sure, honey. You're welcome to try out. Come up and sing a few bars of 'God Bless America.'"

Sarah, gripped suddenly with stage fright, walked slowly toward the front. A wink from Nancy stilled her fears.

"Do you need sheet music?" asked Mrs. Hassell.,

"No, Ma'am. I know the words by heart."

Nancy played a few bars of introduction. Sarah, remembering the words of her choir director at church, took a deep breath. Her voice resonated in the high ceilinged room. She sang with expression to her small audience. Nancy smiled encouragly. When finished, the townspeople clapped with enthusiasm. Sarah returned to her seat, confident she would be given the solo part.

"Thank you, Sarah," said Mrs. Hassell. "You have a lovely deep voice." She turned to the others. "Maxine," she said, "I'd like to hear you."

A lovely brunette with bouncing curls came forward, smiling. Again, Nancy played a few bars of introduction. The young woman's powerful voice filled Sarah with emotions of love and patriotism for her country. She had to blink rapidly to keep tears from spilling. It was no surprise when the director announced Maxine would sing the solo.

As they were leaving, Mrs. Hassell called to Sarah. She hurried over, thinking there may be a part for her in another song. "I'm glad to meet you, Sarah. Tell your grandmother I said hello."

"Yes, Ma'am, I will," answered Sarah, looking expectantly at the director.

"I'd love for you to be a part of the celebration. I can find a place for you in the chorus. You have a deep, clear voice that is perfect for alto notes."

Sarah's smile faded. *Alto!* She didn't sing alto! At church she was always on the front row with the best and strongest sopranos. Altos sat on the back row out of sight. They never got to sing the melody of the beautiful hymns. As a matter of fact, Sarah didn't know what notes they were singing. She did know it was not like anything she had ever heard.

When she got home, the house was still and dark. Stepping inside she hooked the screen door and walked into the living room to turn out the tiny lamp still burning. "How were tryouts?" asked a voice from the shadows.

"Oh, Granny Jewel, you startled me. I didn't know you were still up."

The grandmother stifled a yawn. "I couldn't go to bed until I got a full report."

Sarah plopped down in a chair opposite her grandmother. "It was a waste of time."

"Why do you say that?"

"Because," anger began creeping into the girl's voice. "Even though she let me try out, she already knew who would get the solo parts."

"The important thing is, you tried your best."

"A lady named Maxine got the solo I wanted." Sarah frowned, winding a stray lock of hair around her finger.

"Maxine has an exceptionally beautiful voice with lots of volume."

"Mrs. Hassell thanked me for coming and invited me to be in the chorus."

"That was quite an honor. You're going to join, aren't you?"

"Heck no! I'm not going to waste my time. She said I'd be in the alto section. I'm not about to be stuck behind the sopranos. In Raleigh, I sing on the front row every Sunday." Sarah stuck out her chin. "She'll have to manage without me."

Sarah noted a strange look on her grandmother's face. "Oh, she'll manage very nicely. It's quite an honor to be invited to join the chorus."

"If this is such a great opportunity, why don't you sing? After all, you sing on the front row of St. Paul's choir every Sunday."

"I intend to, my dear. Your grandfather and I will both be singing in the chorus, *and* we were thrilled to be asked."

Sarah stopped twirling her hair and leaned forward. "You were?"

"Of course. Now come sit by me." She patted the flowered cushion and turned the lamp down so only a soft glow partially filled the room. Sarah slid over, sitting close to her grandmother, once again inhaling the soft lilac scent of her perfume. Granny Jewel put an arm around her granddaughter.

"Sarah," she said slowly, "in order for music to have depth and beauty, there must be harmony. If all sang soprano it would be beautiful, but boring. The deep, mellow tones from the second row give beauty, depth and resonance to the melody."

Granny Jewel patted Sarah's arm. "Everything in life must be harmonious." She glanced at the lovely, dark-haired girl beside her, suddenly consumed with such a feeling of love, she had to catch her breath. "Suppose all the birds sang the same song? We could never appreciate the haunting melody of the nightingale. We need the chirp of a sparrow to add contrast. Suppose it was hot weather all year? How could we appreciate a sunny day if there was no rain? If there was no harmony in marriage, many would end in divorce."

Sarah smiled. "I understand, Granny Jewel. I just never thought about things that way."

Jewel Mitchell rose, turned out the light and moved toward the stairs. Sarah followed. "What part do you sing in the chorus, Granny Jewel?"

The grandmother paused on the first step, turned and kissed her granddaughter on the forehead. Giving her a hug, she whispered, "alto."

# Chapter 3

"Well, I'm not one bit surprised," Sarah heard her grandmother's voice as she entered the dining room the following morning

"What are you not surprised about?" asked the girl, giving each grandparent a peck on the cheek.

Granny Jewel struggled to extract pulp from half a grapefruit. Sarah wasn't sure if the frown she wore was from her battle with the fruit, or what she was talking about. She took her seat at the table and waited patiently for her grandmother to continue.

"I'm not one bit surprised Dr. Maxwell put Miriam on strict bed rest until the baby arrives."

Before Sarah could comment, Amy burst in, followed by her mother and Joshua. After greetings, Sarah again turned to her grandmother. "Does that mean she could be in bed a month?"

"A month, more or less. It will be until our new granddaughter decides to make her appearance."

Papa Tom's fork was half way to his lips. He stopped and turned to his wife. "I don't know why you refuse to face facts, Jewel, honey. The baby is a boy, and that's that!"

Jewel Mitchell stabbed the helpless grapefruit with such vigor, the fork handle vibrated. "Dear," she said quietly, "men cannot hope to know about these things; women do."

Amy, jelly and butter from ear to ear, said, "Aunt Miriam's baby is going to be a baby. It won't matter what kind." She waved her spoon much like the way she had seen her beloved Clara do.

"There! Out of the mouths of babes," declared Clara, refilling cups with steaming, savory coffee.

"Sarah," said Papa Tom, "your Uncle Herb and I have talked things over, and we have come up with a plan we hope you will like."

"What is it, Papa?" She felt a sudden rush of satisfaction to know her uncle and grandfather wanted her opinion.

"We sure could use your help at the store, with all the summer visitors in town, but Miriam needs you more. After the baby comes, her parents will be here for a month to help."

"No one can take your mother's place at a time like this," added Granny Jewel.

"I might not be your mama, but you seemed mighty glad to have me around when you took to your child bed," said Clara indignantly.

"That's true," Granny Jewel added hastily. "But, not everyone is fortunate to have a Clara at a time like that."

"I remember the story of how you helped save Mama's life when she was born," said Sarah, softly. The room grew silent for a moment, each remembering.

"How did you save Mama?" asked Joshua, giving Clara a curious look.

"That's a long story, Son, one we'll have to save for a rainy afternoon."

"Granny Jewel, do you still have Clara's apron that mama was wrapped in?"

"Oh, yes, Honey. It's tucked away safely in the cedar chest upstairs."

The front door slammed and Herb Mitchell appeared in the doorway of the dining room. He winked at Sarah and grinned. "Has your grandpa talked to you?" A cup of steaming black coffee was placed in front of him.

"Thanks, Clara," he said gratefully. "I had to make coffee this morning and I believe it curled the edges of the spoon. My dear wife didn't complain, but I could see the hurt in her eyes, as she sipped a few swallows." He glanced at Sarah as he carefully sipped the hot drink. "We need you more with Miriam each day."

"I'll be glad to help any way I can," said Sarah, returning his smile. "But, I hate to know you all are short-handed at the store."

"We think we have that problem solved." Herb Mitchell shifted his gaze to his nephew. "We're offering Joshua a job sweeping, dusting, and putting up stock."

"Wow!" exclaimed the boy, jumping from his chair. "I've got a job! Now I can buy a Red Ryder B-B gun." Suddenly, his face fell. "What am I going to do about Mackie? If I go to work, he won't have anybody to play with."

"Doesn't he help his father paint houses?" asked Uncle Herb.

"Mackie helps his father when he gets home from work."

Father and son exchanged looks. "Well . . .," said Uncle Herb, "we could use him, too. When school starts, he could work Saturdays."

"He'll be too busy to even think about getting in any mischief," added Papa Tom.

Uncle Herb looked at Sarah as he sipped the steaming coffee. "Sarah, I'm going to pay the same as I would if you were at the store."

"Oh, no, Uncle Herb, I don't want pay for helping someone in the family."

"I can't expect you to do it for nothing."

"If Sarah doesn't want her money, I'll be glad to take it," offered Joshua.

"I'm proud my grandson has such a generous spirit," said Papa Tom, grinning.

Sarah hurried toward her aunt's home. The morning sun bore down, making the walk uncomfortable. It was a relief to finally leave the heat of the sidewalk and step up on the wide front porch. Hmmm, the ferns need water and the flowered cushions in the rocking chairs need plumping, and the floor could use a good sweeping. Aunt Miriam has been in bed only a few hours, and already the house is losing its 'woman's touch.'

Before going in, Sarah glanced across the street. Miss Nettie Blackwell and her dog, Barney. were on the front porch. She waved with one hand while watering plants.

Sarah stepped off the porch and hurried across the street, unwilling to announce to the neighborhood her aunt's condition. Soon enough word would get around that Miriam Mitchell had 'took to her bed,' as Clara would say.

"My, Sarah, you look lovely, this morning," said Miss Nettie. "What brings you out so early? Is Miriam all right?"

Sarah knew from the concern written on the older lady's face, she wasn't just being curious, but genuinely concerned. Sarah explained Miriam's present condition, knowing she wouldn't sit beside the telephone all morning, reporting this tidbit of news. All knew Miss Nettie didn't take kindly to idle chatter or gossip. She possessed a wealth of information about most of the people of the small town, all of it safely tucked away, or forgotten over the generations of people she had taught during her teaching career. Likewise, Miss Nettie's occasional dip of sweet snuff was a secret carefully guarded by the people of Beaufort.

"Yoo-hoo," sang Sarah, as she tiptoed across the gleaming hardwood floors of the foyer. The cavernous hallway with ceilings reaching ten feet above the second floor echoed the girl's voice.

An answering, 'yoo-hoo' floated from the spacious upstairs hall. She hurried up the wide stairs, her hand holding the smooth, polished railing. The hard leather soles of her sandals tapped rhythmically on the wooden floor.

"I thought that might be you, Sarah," said her aunt. Sarah paused at the bedroom door. It took several minutes for her eyes to adjust to the darkened room. Flowered drapes and shades at every window were tightly drawn, allowing little light and ventilation to enter.

Sarah stepped over to her aunt's bedside, careful not to bump into a table with a tall lamp and several figurines. She moved closer, taking her aunt's hand.

"Would you like me to bring you something? Uncle Herb told me you can't get out of bed."

"My dear husband thinks I am suddenly an invalid." She squeezed her niece's hand. "I feel fine, but I know how the Hindenburg felt right before it exploded." This attempt brought weak laughter from both. Sarah felt a rush of affection for this lovely woman who had come into their lives after the death of her uncle's first wife.

"Does the air seem a little stuffy?" asked Sarah. An oscillating fan was doing little to stir the stale air. "I could open the windows and let in fresh air." *A few more minutes in here, and I'm going to suffocate,* she thought.

"That's a grand idea, Sarah. Dr. Maxwell told Herb I should rest and remain calm. He did not say I had to be held prisoner in a dark, stuffy room." Miriam fell back against several pillows and stared at the ceiling. "Your uncle is such a worry-wart. He thinks germs are going to fly in the window and attack me."

Sarah hurried over to the tall windows. Each had tiny panes of glass, some with air bubbles or other imperfections. She frowned when she remembered the hours of toil spent scraping putty and old paint from the frames. At the time, she couldn't imagine anyone putting so much effort in restoring such ugly windows. Now, new putty and gleaming white paint on the ornate wooden frames made the windows seem tall and graceful against the pastel plaster walls.

"It's a struggle to open them," said a voice from the bed. "The new paint causes them to stick. Herb says when winter comes, and the heat is on, the wood will shrink and they'll be easier to open. It's the same with half the furniture."

"But Aunt Miriam, who wants their windows open in winter?"

Miriam chuckled. "I started to remind him of that, but he seemed so tense, I didn't say a word."

With effort, Sarah was able to get two windows open. She was rewarded by a rush of cool, salt air off the ocean. Carefully she adjusted the blinds and pushed back the drapes. When she turned, the words she was about to say died in her throat. The woman on the bed faintly resembled her lovely, vivacious aunt. Hair, once glossy dark curls, hung lifeless, pulled back from her face with several bobby pins. Dark circles made her eyes appear sunken. Thankfully, nothing had marred her beautiful smile.

"There! I feel better already!" she said cheerfully. Sarah returned her smile, hoping her expression did not betray the shock she felt. "Would you please prop a pillow behind my back, and one under my ankles. Then, we should be ready for cookies and iced tea.

Sarah hurried to do her aunt's bidding, selecting several soft pillows from a nearby chair. Each was covered with a fine linen pillow case embroidered in flowers and edged in lace. "The pillow cases were wedding presents and gifts made by my friends." Miriam ran her fingers over the delicate handwork. "I regret I never learned the fine art of needlework," she murmured.

"I tried, once, Aunt Miriam, when I was twelve. It seemed like a mild form of torture then. Maybe I was too young."

The aunt smiled. "A girl of seventeen should be busy filling her hope chest with fine linens."

Sarah slid a nearby chair closer to the bed. "Granny Jewel said someday I would have my great-grandmother's linens, so I don't have to worry."

"Have you thought of Amy? She may want some of her great-grandmother's keepsakes. And, if this baby is a girl," Miriam paused and gently patted her tummy, "she will want something that belonged to her great-grandmother."

"I hadn't thought of that. Besides," she said, carefully placing a pillow under her aunt's ankles, "I like the thought of having linens I made. Great Grandmother Frances' handkerchiefs are so old and delicate I'd be afraid they'd blow away if I sneezed on one." Sarah tried to keep alarm from her voice when she saw the size of her aunt's feet and ankles. Before the pregnancy, they had been slender and fine boned, but now were swollen, the skin a strange color.

"Aren't they a sight? When Dr. Maxwell saw them, he ordered me to bed."

Sarah replaced the sheet. "I'll get the refreshments now. She hurried from the room and down the steps. "I know what I'm not going to be," she whispered to herself, "and that would be a nurse. The sick folks of this world are going to have to manage without me."

"Mama," called the girl when she got home. "Where are you, Mama?" she went from room to room in her grandparents' home.

"Your mama walked Amy down to the dime store to find her a new toy," said Clara, busy peeling potatoes. "They should be back any minute."

"I can't wait, Clara. I need to talk to her." Sarah flew through the house, letting the screen door slam behind her.

"Who knows what that child has on her mind now?" Clara asked the potato she was peeling. "She bounces from one crisis to another. I pity the poor man she marries. He'll never know a peaceful moment." Fleetingly, the red haired boy in distant Ohio crossed her mind.

Sarah hurried along the sidewalk toward town. In a few minutes she saw her mother and sister walking slowly toward home.

"What a nice surprise!" said Peggy. "How is Miriam?"

"I have a new ball," cried Amy, holding a gold rubber ball so her big sister could see it.

"That's nice," replied Sarah, absently.

"Mama," she whispered, so Amy couldn't hear her words, "Aunt Miriam looks tired and awful. That was bad enough, but when I saw her feet and ankles, I nearly fainted."

A worried expression crossed her mother's face. "I'll be so relieved when the baby gets here. I've been concerned for her for some time. My brother endured the heartache of losing Louise. Another tragedy in his life would be terrible for him and for us, too." Peggy stopped. She put her hand on Sarah's arm, she whispered, 'Say nothing about this around your grandparents. They are already worried, and this would only make it worse. After supper go to practice for the July 4th celebration and put this from your mind. Lift Miriam and Herb up in your prayers, because that's the best medicine, and the quickest cure for our dear girl."

When the three got home from practice, Sarah saw a note for her by the telephone. She collapsed on the sofa and began reading.

"Phew," exclaimed the grandmother. "I am exhausted. Virginia Hassell is such a hard taskmaster. If we don't hit every note perfectly, we have to do it over."

"Honey," said Papa Tom, "that's why people pack the auditorium when she puts on a production."

"This is a note from Uncle Herb. It says Sadie doesn't work on Wednesdays, and he wants me to come an hour earlier." Sarah tapped a finger on her chin. "Hmmm, I'll go real early and make breakfast for both."

Oh, brother, thought Sarah, searching cabinets. Fixing a meal in someone else' kitchen is an ordeal. When I find a pot we'll have boiled eggs and toast. Of course, I'll have to find the well-hidden toaster.

With Uncle Herb fed and off to Mitchell's grocery, Sarah prepared her aunt's breakfast tray. I'd like to put her boiled egg in a fancy egg cup and a fresh flower in a bud vase, just like in the movies, but her coffee would be frigid by the time I found either.

"Good morning, Sarah," Miriam said cheerfully. "How did you know boiled eggs are my very favorite?" Sarah wondered briefly if this was true, or if her aunt was saying so to make her feel good. One of Miriam Mitchell's many talents was saying things to make people feel good.

Sarah, smiling, answered, "The frying pan was hiding, so I had to adjust the menu. Now I know why Clara refers to our kitchen as 'my kitchen.' It's because she has everything hidden where only she can find it."

Breakfast over, Miriam slid the tray aside. She looked at Sarah and smiled a tired smile. "Now, Sarah, we have a long, hot day ahead. What do you propose we do to pass the time?"

Again, the girl felt a rush of pleasure that an adult was asking her opinion. She adjusted the pillows behind her aunt's back and under her ankles. Smoothing the sheets, she answered, "I told my friend, Nancy Russert about my new job. She is so anxious to come for a visit."

"I hope you told her to come any time."

"As a matter of fact," continued the girl, "she'll be here this morning. She wants so much to see you." Sarah rolled her eyes. "I think she is bringing her needlework."

Miriam looked doubtful. "Well, Sarah, I suppose we'll soon know if the ability to sew is one of God's gifts to us."

"I'm afraid He may have passed me by when He was giving out that talent," replied Sarah.

"Now, Sarah, we mustn't take that attitude. We will be defeated before we begin," said her aunt in her best teaching voice.

"Yes, Ma'am." Sarah turned to adjust the window shade to block the fierce morning sun. *Humph, she hasn't poked herself with a needle as many times as I have.*

Breakfast dishes washed, Sarah left the kitchen. "Yoo-hoo," came a soft voice from the foyer.

"Come in," Sarah answered. She stepped into the front hall and saw her friend Nancy standing inside the screen door. She was wearing a starched cotton dress, white socks and sandals. Matching barrettes tried vainly to tame stubborn curls. A flowered tote bag was clutched in her hands. Sarah knew the bag contained pins, embroidery thread and bits of fabric. It also held other mysterious implements of torture only Nancy understood. She knew with a sinking heart that soon contents of the bag would be spread across her aunt's bed, Miriam a captive to Nancy's patient, thorough instruction.

"I hope I'm not intruding," whispered the visitor, rolling her eyes in the direction of the upstairs bedroom.

"No, no, not at all," answered Sarah, smiling. "Aunt Miriam will be happy to have company. I'm afraid she gets bored with just me to talk to."

"Good morning, Nancy," greeted Miriam Mitchell. "What a nice surprise."

"Good morning, Mrs. Mitchell," whispered Nancy. She stepped over and laid her tote bag on the foot of the bed. "Sarah called last night and told me you all were becoming bored. I brought along things we'll need to get you started doing needlework." She cast an accusing glance at her friend. "I haven't had much luck with your niece, but I haven't given up. Someday I know she'll be able to turn a fine seam."

Nancy began emptying the overstuffed bag. There was a card of several needles with large eyes. "These needles are made especially for embroidery floss since it is thicker than regular thread." Sarah noticed her aunt showing interest in the treasures from Nancy's bag. I must plan my escape, or soon my determined friend will have me cornered. She went to a window to adjust the shade. The cool ocean breeze bore sounds from the outside. Occasionally, a boat horn would signal the drawbridge. The wailing siren acknowledged the boat's request, and slowly the span opened, allowing the boat passage. Neighbors called friendly greetings across fences. Faint squeals of laughter by children swimming in Taylor's Creek also punctuated the morning air.

Before she turned away, her attention was drawn to her uncle, hurrying along the sidewalk, carrying a large cardboard box.

"Aunt Miriam, Uncle Herb is coming up the walk, carrying a box. I'll go downstairs and hold the door for him."

"Sarah, you're not going to get away that easily," called Nancy as Sarah fled the room.

"Do you need some help, Uncle Herb?" asked Sarah, holding the screen door.

"No, honey, it's not that heavy. I just need to get it upstairs for your aunt. I think it's the very thing she has been waiting and looking for." Sarah, consumed with curiosity, followed closely.

"I hope this is what I think it is," said Miriam brightly. "Put it right here." She swept sewing supplies aside with one hand. The girls stood back, impatient to learn the contents of the mysterious box.

"No, no, my dear. This box has been in the post office and on trucks, and may have germs. I'll open it on the cedar chest." He produced a small knife, cut the twine and tape holding the box, and carefully reached inside. All watched as he removed soft bundles wrapped in crisp, white tissue paper and placed them in his wife's hands.

"Girls, come and see," whispered Miriam. As the tissue was folded back, all stared at tiny, soft garments. "Mama and my sisters have been busy preparing a layette for the baby. Some of the clothes are new, and some are hand-me-downs from my sister's children." She continued unwrapping bundles, amazed at the tiny garments.

"Well, girls, I have to get back to work," announced Herb Mitchell, shattering the spell. "I'll leave you ladies to tend to my child's wardrobe."

Sarah followed her uncle out to the hall. "Uncle Herb, do you think the baby is a boy or girl?"

"Sarah, honey," he said, pausing on the steps, "it doesn't matter one little bit. I'm like Amy. The baby is going to be a baby, and that's good enough for me."

When Sarah returned to the bedroom, she was puzzled to see Nancy frown with each garment she picked up. "What's the matter, Nancy. You look worried."

In a prim voice, Nancy said, "These clothes are wonderfully made, but there is no trim. You expect baby clothes to have flowers or baby ducks embroidered on the sleeve or hem. There is no satin ribbon or lace on a single garment."

"You're right, Nancy. This is a very special baby. Our whole family, plus half the high school and most of the townspeople are waiting." Sarah looked across the bed, her eyes meeting Nancy's. "What can we do?"

Miriam patted the mound under the sheet. "This baby can't wait while Nancy embroiders each tiny piece. That would take till Christmas."

Nancy thought a moment, clasped her hands over her heart, and exclaimed, "I have the answer, Mrs. Mitchell." Sarah and Miriam stared in silence. "I can't tell, because I want it to be a surprise." She began to hastily stuff cloth, needles, thread and pins in the oversized bag. Sarah felt a sense of relief as she saw the instruments of torture disappear. "I'll be back tomorrow, nice and early. There is much to do."

"Can you give us a hint?" called Sarah, following her friend to the front door.

Nancy gave a sly smile. "Only one thing. Be sure to have plenty of lemonade and cookies on hand."

# Chapter 4

The sound of footsteps on the porch was heard the next morning, followed by giggles and whispers. "Aunt Miriam, I think your surprise is here," announced Sarah. She hurried downstairs to answer a timid knock.

"Sarah," whispered Nancy, her nose pressed against the screen, "I brought reinforcements." Behind her friend stood the Young Ladies' Sewing Circle, anxious to get a peek at their beloved teacher's home. Sarah recognized several from Sunday school.

Peggy Jones, the tallest, was standing at the back of the wide porch. She whispered something to the twins, Sue and Dianna, sending them into gales of laughter. "Hush, you two," ordered Catherine, her large brown eyes darting from girl to girl, giving each a disapproving look.

"Gwen started it," said Evelyn, pouting.

"I did not! You try to blame everything on me. When I get home . . ."

Mary Vann blocked the door. The oldest in the group, all deferred to her commands. "Girls, this is serious. Now calm down, or I won't open the door. We are on a mission and there is *no* time to waste." The note of authority in her voice was not lost on the group.

"Your big sister is too bossy," whispered Dianna in Evelyn's ear, careful to not be overheard by Mary Vann.

Evelyn, the younger sister, stepped closer to Dianna. "You think this is bad? You should see her at home. She tells me what to do all day."

Sarah swung the door open. "Welcome, girls. Nancy promised Aunt Miriam a surprise, but we never guessed it would be this exciting." The girls followed Sarah through the hall and up the wide staircase, their chatter silenced as they admired the handsome old house.

"Come in, everyone," welcomed Miriam Mitchell. Hair in a neat roll on the back of her neck, and fresh makeup helped the aunt regain her former beauty. "Please have a seat, and tell me what you have been doing since school closed."

Even though in bed, dressed in a soft, cool nightgown and robe, Miriam Mitchell was very much in charge. Sarah watched her aunt's eyes sparkle, a ready smile for each. All returned the smile so freely given, eyes riveted on their teacher.

*Aunt Miriam is suddenly different,* observed Sarah. *The girls have given her an energy she lacked before they arrived.* Sitting on the window seat, she watched the girls inch closer, eager to share experiences. *What is her secret?* wondered Sarah. *We all have classes we can barely endure, teachers we don't like. There is something different happening here. I'll have to ask Miss Nettie. Everyone in Beaufort loves her and remembers being in her class.*

"And who is this pretty girl?" asked Miriam, interrupting Sarah's thoughts. "I don't believe we've met." Before the girl could answer, Nancy Russert spoke.

"Forgive my bad manners, Mrs. Mitchell. This is Lillian Lawrence. She moved here this summer, because her daddy is in the Marine Corps, and is stationed at Cherry Point."

"Welcome, Lillian, dear. You look so much like my college roommate. She was little and cute, like you. I know the girls are glad to have you join their sewing circle. This lively group can surely keep you from getting homesick."

"Now tell me," said Miriam, "to what do we owe the pleasure of your visit? Is it a special occasion?"

Once more Nancy Russert took charge. "Mrs. Mitchell, your mother and sisters made lovely, delicate clothes for your baby, but they are *too plain*. We would like to embroider lambs, and flowers and ducks on each. We can dress up some pieces with satin ribbon and lace." The girls stared at their former teacher, waiting an answer.

"What a lovely thing to do!" The woman's eyes sparkled with unshed tears. Helen, a tall, slender girl with brown hair and blue eyes, moved toward the bed.

"Mrs. Mitchell," she asked shyly, "may we see the baby's room?"

"Oh, yes! Sarah, please take the girls to the nursery." The girls abandoned their sewing baskets, anxious to see where the baby would sleep.

In the hall, Sarah turned and addressed the group. "The nursery is located in the next room. If the baby cries at night, the parents will hear. Also, this bedroom is the smallest of the three, so it seemed the best choice."

"Oh, Sarah, you sound like a tour guide at the Smithsonian," said Peggy. "Just show us the room before we die of suspense."

"Stop being a grump," whispered Evelyn, poking Peggy in the ribs. "If Sarah feels important, it's because she is." Following Sarah, the girls filed silently into the next room. No one spoke while each looked at every detail. Both windows had shades of creamy white, same as the walls. Snow white Priscilla curtains made of sheer organdy criss-crossed the tall windows, letting soft light filter through. A crib and matching dresser ordered from Eastman Furniture in Morehead City lined two walls, a bassinette stood ready against the third. A dainty rocking chair from his parents' attic had been painted by the expectant father. On the polished hardwood floor a rug of pastel hues added color. A shelf under the bassinette held stacks of soft cotton diapers, folded and ready.

"The room smells like vanilla," said Lillian, "and reminds me of vanilla ice cream."

"I can't wait to get grown and have a baby so I can fix a room like this," whispered Evelyn to her sister.

"Humph, you'll have to find yourself a husband first," retorted Mary Vann.

"Men don't like bossy women, so she may be married before you," came a voice from the back of the room.

"Who said that?" demanded Mary Vann, scanning each innocent face.

"Girls, this isn't helping us accomplish our mission. Time is of the essence," said Nancy Russert in a crisp voice.

At noon, Herb Mitchell's face appeared at the door of the bedroom. His eyes widened when he saw girls in chairs, on the window seat, at the foot of the bed, and some seated on the floor, surrounded by needles, hoops, and thread. He gave a quick greeting and backed away from the door.

"Hello, Uncle Herb," greeted Sarah, escaping from the room.

"Sarah, what's going on? It looks like a busy day at the shirt factory."

"It's the Young Ladies' Sewing Circle."

"Are you a member?"

"Do I look that desperate?" Sarah shrugged her shoulders. "They're embroidering trim on the layette. Nancy thinks the baby clothes from New York are too plain."

Herb Mitchell started for the steps. "I'm getting ready to make sandwiches for lunch. You're welcome to eat with us," offered Sarah. Eyes widening, he shook his head vigorously. "No-o-o, I wouldn't want to interrupt. I appreciate what the girls are doing. It's very sweet of them. However, I think I'll go to Mama's for lunch." Hurrying down the stairs, he called over his shoulder, "I'll be home the usual time." The screen door slammed behind him as he hurried from the house.

Sarah leaned over the banister rail. *He'll do that once after the baby comes,* thought Sarah, *and never again.* Lively music from the victrola and radio would also be silenced. Babies had a way of changing everything, without even trying. *You're changing their diaper, and they're changing your whole life.*

By four-thirty, each tiny garment was trimmed in delicate designs and patterns. "Girls, I can never thank you enough," said Miriam, close to tears. "In years to come, I'll show my child the lovely work you've done today. Each piece will be a keepsake."

"Oh, Mrs. Mitchell, you'll have so many children, these clothes will be worn out."

"No, no, not a houseful, but, maybe one more. Two children seems an ideal number." As they filed out, all promised to return for a visit when the baby arrived. Miriam collapsed against a bank of soft pillows. "Sarah, I wouldn't be more weary if I had been ironing all day."

"Get some rest before Uncle Herb comes home. If he sees you're exhausted, he may declare no visitors until after the baby gets here."

Miriam rubbed her broad tummy and said, "The baby, the baby, that's all we can say. I'll be so happy when we can say 'he' or 'she.'"

"At our house, Amy is the only one who says, 'the baby.' Granny Jewel and Papa Tom argue all day over what the baby will be. She says *she,* and he says *he,* and neither will budge."

At five o'clock, Herb Mitchell returned, relieved to learn the girls left at four-thirty. When Sarah said goodbye, he was sitting on the foot of the bed, examining each tiny garment.

Sarah stepped out on the front porch, careful not to let the door slam behind her. "Five o'clock and it's still hot as a furnace." She sighed, dreading the hot walk to her grandparents' home. Looking across the street, she saw Miss Nettie and Barney sitting on the porch. She waved when she saw Sarah. Crossing the deserted street, Sarah stepped up on the porch. "I need to ask you a question, Miss Nettie. I can't think of anyone more qualified to answer it."

"Settle yourself in this rocking chair next to mine, and fire away," said the older woman.

Sarah noticed her friend looked cool and refreshed, even in the late afternoon heat. The odor of delicate cologne reached Sarah. *She smells good, just like my granny,* thought Sarah. Barney, eager for a pat on the head, looked expectantly at their guest.

"Now Sarah, if it's matters of the heart, I'm afraid I won't be much help. My intended, Owen Nance, lost his life on the battlefield in World War I."

"I know, Miss Nettie. But, my granny told me lots of young men wanted to be your beau." Sarah smiled at the slender woman who still retained much of her youthful beauty.

"Perhaps you're right, my dear, but my heart belongs to Owen, and his memory." She grew silent, staring across the street. Sarah knew she was not seeing her aunt's house, but was reliving a time long past. Sarah remained silent, not wanting to shatter the woman's reverie.

After a few moments, Miss Nettie turned to Sarah. "Now, my dear," she said brightly, "what is your question? I'll be glad to help you if I can."

"Yes, ma'am. I want to know why a group of girls, all different, feel the same toward Aunt Miriam. They squabble among themselves, but the mention of her name, and they all get that worshipful look. I love her, sure, she's my aunt—I'm supposed to love her. What does she do to win such adoring looks?"

The woman was silent so long, Sarah started to ask again. "Sarah," she finally said, "Miriam treats each of her students with respect and love. Her feelings are sincere, and the students know it. The feeling is so powerful, none can prevail against it, even the 'bad boys'. She believes each of her students has exceptional abilities, and none want to disappoint her. She makes them feel good about themselves." Miss Nettie leaned toward Sarah, and smiled. "Love is the magic ingredient," she whispered.

Sarah sat quietly, digesting this information. She thought of all her teachers over the years. Some were OK, and some she'd follow to the end of the earth.

Walking home, Sarah deliberately slowed her step. Shade from the huge elms sheltered her from the sun's penetrating rays. *What would it be like to have people love you that you weren't even kin to? If you were a teacher, every day you would go to school and share new ideas with a classroom of children. You could discover things together and there would be laughter, lots of laughter, and of course, the secret ingredient.* A new feeling began to stir deep inside the lovely girl.

"Aunt Clara, Aunt Clara," called a voice at the back door of the Mitchell home. Strong knuckles rapped on the wooden frame. Clara, setting the table for breakfast, hurried to the kitchen.

"John Ramus, are you trying to wake the dead? Keep your voice down, or you will wake the whole family."

"I don't mean to wake the family, just Joshua. I got something to show him."

"Well, that boy hasn't stirred. You'll have to come back later."

The look of disappointment on her tall nephew's face surprised the woman. *Now what have those two cooked up?* she wondered.

"I'll sit right here on the top step and wait," replied John Ramus, his jaw set in a firm line. Clara realized he was not going to disappear, so she poured a cup of hot coffee and handed it to the young man.

"You got a stubborn streak a mile long, Ramie."

"I know that, Aunt Clara." Seeing that his aunt was not armed with her stirring spoon, he continued, "Who do you suppose I got it from?"

"Now, don't you get sassy with me, young man, or . . ."

"Ramie!" A young voice pierced the air. "I didn't know you were here!" Joshua burst through the screen door, and sat close to his friend.

Clara remained at the door, hands on hips. "Get up from there, boy and come eat your breakfast. Whatever Ramie's got to say can wait."

"Go on now, Joshua. We don't want to rile my Aunt Clara."

"Ramie needs some breakfast," said the boy, not moving.

"Ramie can take care of himself," answered Clara, impatiently.

"He looks mighty empty to me, Clara."

"I'm not going to stand at this door all day arguing with the two of you." She held the door open. "Joshua Bowers, come in here and get to the table. I'll see Ramie gets something to eat. Mind me now, or I'll pull my stirring spoon out of that pot of grits."

Breakfast over, Joshua returned to the porch. The man had finished breakfast and was enjoying a cigarette.

"Blow a smoke ring, Ramie," begged Joshua, returning to his place beside his friend. Being able to execute perfect rings of smoke was a large part of the reason Joshua held the man in such high regard. After putting his finger through several rings, Ramie turned to Joshua. "I got a package in the mail yesterday."

"Who from?"

"From the Veteran's Administration."

"What was it, Ramie?"

Ramie glanced at his little friend and smiled.

"You'd never guess in a million years."

"Was it a box of medals?"

Ramie leaned closer. "Better than that. It's a new leg."

Joshua's eyes widened. "You got a new leg?"

"Yep." Another perfect smoke ring.

Rings forgotten, Joshua asked, "Why did you get a new leg? Did you wear out the old one? Did it get too small, just like clothes?"

Ramie laughed. "No, Joshua, I didn't wear it out, or outgrow it. They sent me a better one. Would you like to see it?"

Joshua's eyes rested on Ramie's pant leg. "You bet I would!"

Ramie slowly rolled up his right pant leg. "Wow!" exclaimed the boy, admiring the artificial limb. Suddenly a frown crossed his face.

"What's the matter," asked Ramie, puzzled.

"It's not the right color. Your skin is brown, and that leg is pink."

"It's the only color it comes in. It's made of a brand new material called plastic, and I don't care if it's purple. This leg doesn't weigh as much, and it's easy to keep clean."

"I didn't know you had to bathe artificial legs, too." When Ramie stopped laughing, Joshua was ready with his next question. "What are you going to do with the old one?"

"Hmmm, I haven't given it any thought. I guess I'll keep it as a spare."

"You probably won't ever need it again."

"Yeah, I hope I never have to drag that thing again, although it's better than crutches."

Joshua rested his hand on Ramie's knee. "You know, Ramie," he began, "that old leg is only going to be in the way." He waited a moment, then flashed the smile that always melted his mama's heart. "I know a *good* thing to do with it."

Ramie glanced down at his little pal. "What would that be?"

"You could give it to *me*."

Ramie smiled. "What would a fellow with two good legs want with another?"

Joshua thought for a moment. "My mama says two heads are better than one. Maybe three legs are better than two."

Ramie let out a howl of laughter and slapped his other knee. "It's yours! "Anybody who can think of an answer that fast, deserves an extra appendage." "But," Ramie's face clouded, "What are your grandparents and your mama going to say?"

Joshua's eyes sparkled. "My granny won't mind."

"How about the rest of the family?"

"Granny Jewel is the boss," he whispered. "If she says it's all right, then I don't have to worry."

"I should say not! The very idea!" Peggy Bowers stared across the dinner table at her son. Joshua quickly looked at his grandmother for support. Seeing shock written on her face, he glanced at his grandfather. He was staring at his plate, briskly stirring food that was in no need of stirring.

"Sarah, help me," he implored.

"Uh, why don't you ask Clara, little brother? She may think it should stay in the family like a, uh, a keepsake."

Before he could speak, Clara appeared in the doorway, wiping her hands on a flowered apron. "I got nothing to say, cause I can't believe what I'm hearing."

The grandfather slowly raised his head. "This is more serious than I realized. For the first time in almost fifty years, Clara has *nothing* to say. That's scary."

"I got plenty I could say to you, but there are children present." Shaking her head, she turned and disappeared.

"Mama, you want me to get good grades in school. Ramie's leg could help."

"I can hardly wait to hear what's coming next," said his mother.

"Well-l-l-l," Joshua looked at each family member, all waiting. He took a deep breath. "If we have to do a project on World War ll, other kids will bring German lugers, medals, Japanese swords and foreign money. I'll be the only one there with an artificial leg."

Joshua's logic was met with silence. Large tears formed as he voiced his final plea. "Mama, you're always telling us to never, *never* hurt another person's feelings—no matter what. If Ramie thinks you don't like his leg, his feelings will be hurt." A tear spilled, ran down his cheek and splashed on his shirt.

Papa Tom cleared his throat. "You know, Sweetheart . . ."

"Don't say it, Thomas," interrupted his wife. "I already know what you're leading to."

Papa Tom straightened, wearing a stern look. "Jewel dear, I am the head of this household, and I sit at the head of this table." To Sarah, it seemed her grandmother began to shrink before their eyes. "Ramie came home from the war and people were embarrassed to speak of his injury, and even avoided him. When we were in the shed, working on the outboard motor, he spoke of how many times he'd had his feelings hurt. He said Joshua was the only person who was not afraid to talk openly. Ramie also said he never felt self conscious, and could relax around him." Papa Tom paused and cleared his throat. "I'm proud to know Ramie is willing to entrust his artificial leg to my grandson."

The silence was broken by Joshua's mother. "It's *not* coming to Raleigh."

"That's fine, Peggy. If Joshua needs it for a history lesson, I'll get in the car and drive it to Raleigh myself. In the meantime, it can stay here in case Ramie needs it."

"You can keep it in your closet, dear," offered the grandmother. "It will be safe there," she added.

"It would look good on the mantle in my bedroom."

"*On the mantle?*"

"Yes, Granny. You have a big wooden goose over the fireplace in the living room."

"It is a swan decoy, carved by Curt Salter of Harker's Island."

"Why do you keep it there? It would be safer in a closet."

"I want it where I can see it every day, because it is beautiful and has great sentimental value. It was carved by someone whose talent and ability I admire and respect." For a moment neither spoke. Finally, without taking her eyes from her grandson's, she said, "I understand now, Joshua. After breakfast, I'll clear the mantle in your room."

# Chapter 5

Before daybreak, the strident ringing of the telephone shattered the silence of the Mitchell household.

"Yes, yes, I hear you," mumbled Granny Jewel, springing from bed on the first ring. She grabbed a light housecoat as she rounded the foot of the four-poster bed, not pausing long enough to search for slippers.

"Be careful, dear," advised her husband, turning over and finding a more comfortable position.

Not pausing long enough to fasten her robe, the woman clutched the front against her, sash streaming behind.

"Hello, hello," she whispered, not wanting to awaken the rest of the family.

"Jewel, is that you?"

Jewel Mitchell recognized the soft voice of her long time friend. "Yes, Nettie, it's me. What time is it?" Granny Jewel squinted at the clock on the living room wall. It was still too dark to see the hands.

"Well, it's almost four o'clock, dear."

"Is anything wrong?" concern was in the grandmother's voice.

"Now, you know I'm not one to gossip, or spread tales. I pride myself on minding my own business."

"I know that, Nettie, and it's quite a wonderful trait." Granny Jewel rolled her eyes, trying to remain calm. She knew in good time her friend would reveal the reason for her early morning call.

"Barney woke me a short time ago, and wanted to go out to be excused. He doesn't do this often, only if he has had a lot of water to drink."

"Yes, Nettie," said Granny Jewel, tapping her long finger nails on the hall table.

"While I waited for Barney to do his, uh, business, the lights came on in Herb's house. First the bedroom light, then the bathroom and soon the hall light. I declare, Jewel, I never saw a house so lit up. You understand now, I wasn't spying."

The grandmother clutched the telephone, her knuckles white. "What happened then, Nettie?"

"A few minutes later, I'm not sure how long, it could have been as much as five minutes . . ."

"Nettie Blackwell, if you don't get to the point, I'm going to reach through this telephone, and pull your hair!"

"Well, Jewel, you don't have to get so huffy," replied the friend.

"I'm sorry, Nettie. Please continue." Jewel Mitchell knew from years of friendship, that Nettie Blackwell could not be rushed.

"As I was about to say, Herb came rushing out and started the car, rushed back and got Miriam. The poor dear! She was barely able to stand, much less walk! After Herb helped her into the car, he hurried back to get the suitcase. I guess in the excitement, he forgot it. Anyway, they drove off down the street, lickity-split." Miss Nettie paused and took a deep breath. "I went over, turned off the lights and closed the front door."

"Thank you, Nettie. I really appreciate what you've done. We'll get dressed and go over to the hospital."

"Call me when you know something."

Granny Jewel hung up, forgetting to say goodbye.

"Tom, Peggy, everybody get up. Herb took Miriam to the hospital, and there isn't a minute to lose!" She clutched the thin robe and hurried upstairs.

"Tom Mitchell, you're still in bed!" she exclaimed from the doorway. She grabbed the corner of the sheet covering her husband and gave it a mighty yank. "We have to go to the hospital, *now!*"

Papa Tom sat up, his hair in a tangle and tried to focus. "Jewel, honey," he said blinking, "we're not going anywhere; not yet, anyway. When Herb has some news, I'm sure we'll be the first to know."

Peggy appeared in the doorway, her eyes bright. "Today's the day, Mama. You're going to have a June grandbaby. There can be birthday parties in the backyard, and someday, your granddaughter can have her wedding on her birthday."

"Peggy, maybe we'd better get her born, *before* we get her married."

"My grandson isn't going to care what month he ties the knot."

"It isn't a boy, I tell you, Tom!"

"Is, too."

"Is not!"

"Stop arguing, you two," admonished their daughter. "I'll call Mary Stewart and have her come and get Amy and Joshua. They're too young to visit anyone in the hospital. We could leave them with Sarah, but she should go with us since she has been Miriam's companion."

The grandfather stood, stretching his full six feet. "We're not going anywhere, so be calm. Let's go downstairs and put on a pot of coffee, because there won't be any more sleeping in this house tonight, or this morning, or whatever time it is."

55

Granny Jewel stood her ground. "Herb is my son. He'll need his mother."

"He's my son, too, and he'll call if he needs his mother."

Dressing hastily, the family gathered in the living room. Joshua and Amy curled up on the sofa. Sarah joined them, propped in a nearby chair.

"June 28, 1949, the day of my granddaughter Emma's birth," murmured Granny Jewel between sips of steaming black coffee.

"Soon, very soon, you'll see I was right all along. June 28, 1949, is the birthday of my grandson, Eli."

At seven thirty, Clara stuck her head in the back door. "Oh, Lord, what has happened? Is somebody dead?"

"No, Clara," said Jewel Mitchell, hugging her lifelong friend. "Miriam is in the hospital, and *my husband* refuses to go over and wait with Herb."

"Hum-m-m, seems like the next best thing is a big breakfast. With bacon and eggs under our belts, we can face anything." Clara, tying a clean apron around her waist, reached in the cabinet for the iron frying pan.

"Can we *please* have pancakes?" begged Joshua. "I know they're only for special days, like Sunday, but this is a special day. I'm going to have a first cousin!"

While strips of bacon were sizzling in the pan, Clara mixed ingredients for light, fluffy pancakes.

"I'm going to make another pot of coffee, Clara. You can't have too much strong, hot coffee at a time like this." stated Granny Jewel whirling around in the middle of the kitchen floor.

Sarah and Amy were assigned the setting of the table. "I'm going to use the brightest, prettiest table cloth in the buffet drawer," announced Sarah.

"Me, too," agreed Amy.

When the last golden pancake and strip of crisp bacon were gone, Granny Jewel leaped to her feet and began furiously scraping plates.

"Honey, if you're not careful, you'll scrape the flowers off," declared Papa Tom. "Nothing you can do will make the telephone ring. Sarah can help Clara, we'll go sit in the living room and wait."

"Tom, you know I can't sit quietly and wait. I'll scream. I need to be busy." She headed for the kitchen, carrying a stack of plates.

Kitchen shining, and every pot and pan put away, there was nothing to do but sit and wait. Sarah sat on the window seat watching the sky turn from purple to pale blue. *Another scorcher*, she decided. The grandparents sat on the sofa, holding hands. Peggy entertained Amy with a picture book, and Joshua dozed in an easy chair. Clara, looking undisturbed, was busily twisting the hem of her apron.

The ringing of the telephone split the silence. "I'll get it!" everyone cried.

"No!" boomed the grandfather. "*I'll get it!*" No one argued as he crossed the room and stepped into the hall.

"Hello," he said. For several painful moments, Papa Tom said nothing while the family ached to hear his next words.

"I knew it!" he cried. "I told your mother all along the baby was a boy, but she didn't believe me." Again he paused, as the family squealed and danced about the room.

"What's that, Son?" The room was suddenly silent. "You want to speak to your mama? Sure, she's right here." All eyes were on the grandmother as she hurried into the hall and took the telephone.

"Herb, darling, it's your mama," she said softly. After what seemed endless moments, she looked up into her husband's blue eyes. "A *girl?* A baby girl, you say? Your father announced the baby was a boy."

More endless moments. "One each? Two babies? Your grandfather and I were both right! How is Miriam? Are the babies all right? How much did they weigh?" Can we come over now?"

"Jewel, Honey, give him time to answer," said Papa Tom, his arm around her shoulder. Finally the grandmother lowered the receiver and looked in the living room. "Miriam wants to speak to Sarah," she said, eyes misting.

"Me?" asked the girl. She was holding Amy and quickly thrust her in Peggy's open arms. She took the receiver from her grandmother. "Hello," she said softly.

"Sarah," her Aunt said softly. "Thank you for taking such good care of me. The babies, Emma and Eli, are perfect, and want to meet their aunt."

"We'll all be there this afternoon when they show the babies, and Aunt Miriam, I love you!"

"I know you do, you showed it every day, and Sarah, I love you, too."

Clara, whose apron resembled an accordion, was wringing her hands. "What are they going to do? There's only enough diapers and clothes for *one* baby. And, there's only one crib."

"Don't you worry your head one bit, Clara," announced Papa Tom. "No Mitchell baby has had to sleep on the floor yet. By the time the new mama gets home, we'll have another crib in the nursery, and enough clothes for both."

At the end of ten days, the Mitchell nursery had two matching white cribs. Eastman Furniture rushed an order to the manufacturer, and in record time, one was assembled and delivered. The baby department in Upton's Department store on Front Street had shelves bare to the wall. A birdseye diaper could not be found anywhere in the town of

Beaufort. All were washed and folded in the Mitchell nursery, waiting for the newest members of the family.

The new father, having lunch with his parents, looked tired and worn.

"Son, one baby is hard work, two will be toil."

"I know, Mama. Still, it may be easier having them home. Working all day and rushing to the hospital until visiting hours are over, is very tiring." He looked at his niece. "Sarah, would you mind keeping your regular hours? Miriam won't be confined to the bed, so between the two of you, they can be fed and diapered. With Sadie doing the cooking, we should do fine. Miriam's parents are coming for several weeks, and they can help, too."

"You haven't left a thing for your mother to do. I declare, I feel left out."

"Oh, Mama, don't say that." Herb rushed over and gave his mother a hug. "You're the person I rely on most. When summer is over, Sarah will return to Raleigh, Miriam's parents will go back to New York, and we would be lost without you."

Granny Jewel smiled at her son. "You know your father and I will do anything we can." The new father looked relieved.

No more than the tide can be stopped from coming in Taylor's Creek twice every day, could the tide of visitors and well wishers be kept from flooding the Mitchell residence for days after the newest members arrived home.

Each morning Emma and Eli were bathed, dressed and brought downstairs, ready to receive guests. Sarah held Emma, while Miriam held Eli. Sadie was in charge of warming bottles and fixing lunch. A stack of snow-white diapers was kept on the dresser in the downstairs bathroom, to avoid extra trips to the nursery.

"Mom and Dad called last night," Miriam said brightly. "I haven't seen them since our wedding, and I miss them. One of my sisters is coming."

"There was so much going on during the wedding, I hardly remember them," said Sarah. "Which of your four sisters is coming?"

"Harriet, the unmarried sister. She still lives at home, the poor dear."

Sarah was curious about her aunt's remark. Before the week was out, the reason for the remark was all too evident.

Two days later, a car carrying a New York license plate slowed and stopped in front of the Mitchell home. Three weary adults slowly climbed out, stretched and looked up at the tall, gracious home.

"Hummm," murmured the older woman. "The outside is just as Miriam described it. Let's see what the inside looks like." With the other two following obediently, Miriam's mother hurried up the steps and advanced on the front door. She banged on the frame and waited.

"Come in," called a familiar voice.

The twins' other grandmother swung the door open and stepped inside. "Miriam, is that you? Why didn't you answer the door?" The older woman stepped in the living room as Miriam handed Eli to Sarah.

"Mama! Daddy!" she cried, embracing her parents. "And sweet sister Harriet." She gave her sister an extra long hug. "Come and see the babies," she said proudly, stepping aside.

Ruth Thompson was across the room in three steps. "Miriam, it's not safe for one so young to hold both babies." She scooped one in her arms. "And who might this be?" she asked, studying the face of the sleeping baby.

"Oh, Mama, that's Emma. Isn't she beautiful?" Miriam's eyes shone with love and pride.

"She looks a little puny to me, Miriam. Is she getting enough to eat?"

Sarah, clutching Eli, watched her beloved aunt shrink from her mother's harsh words.

"Harriet, come here and get this baby. I don't think he's safe in the arms of one so young."

Miriam, trying to ease a painful situation, said, "Mama, you remember Sarah. She's Herb's niece and a bridesmaid at our wedding."

"Hello, dear," the woman said absently. "Miriam, where are our rooms? Your father needs to unpack the car." From her vantage point in the middle of the room, Ruth Thompson's eyes roved, missing nothing. Finally, they settled on Sarah. "Hop up, Dearie, and let me sit there. I'll take the baby, and you can hurry on home."

Sarah's eyes darted to her aunt. It was as if her face was crumbling. Knowing her aunt was uncomfortable, she stood and handed Eli to his grandmother.

"I'll walk you to the door, Sarah," said her aunt. Stepping on the porch, Miriam whispered, "Sarah, please forgive my mother's rude behavior. It's not just you. She talks like that to everybody. You probably wondered why I moved so far from home. Now you know."

"It's fine, Aunt Miriam. There's plenty for me to do at home. Clara always needs help in the kitchen."

"You're a wonderful girl, a perfect niece and a treasured friend."

Sarah hugged her aunt. "Let me know when the coast is clear," she whispered.

"*Miriam*! Are you going to stand on the porch all day? These babies need attention, and somebody needs to start dinner. I'm starving!" This was Sarah's cue to dart down the steps and head for home.

'Sarah, darling, why are you home early? Is anything wrong?" asked Granny Jewel anxiously.

"Where is Mama, Granny Jewel?" asked Sarah, ignoring her grandmother's question.

"She's upstairs giving Amy a bath. The child has been slaving over a hot puddle making mud pies."

"I'll bet she's as proud of her recipes as Clara." A smile flitted across the girl's face.

"She's had help today," added the grandmother, following Sarah. "Mary came over with Laney, and I declare, those little girls did have fun." She paused a moment. "You haven't answered my question. Is anything wrong?" She followed her granddaughter into the bathroom.

Amy was happily playing in several inches of warm water, her mother sitting on the side of the tub. Sarah stepped in, nearly filling the tiny space. Granny Jewel, close behind, slid inside with barely enough room to close the door.

"What's up?" asked Peggy, beginning to worry.

"Miriam's parents and older sister are here."

"That's fine, dear." The grandmother patted her on the shoulder.

"I suppose," said the girl doubtfully.

"Here," a voice from the hall interrupted. "What's going on in there? In case you haven't noticed, that's a bathroom, not a conference room. Either let me in, or talk loud enough for me to hear with my ear to the door."

Granny Jewel pushed against Sarah, wedging her against the sink, and opened the door a tiny crack. She peered out with one eye. "Clara, there's no more room . . ."

"Of course there is." Clara pushed against the door, forcing the grandmother to sit on the commode lid. "There," she said with satisfaction. "I knew there was room for one more. Now, what did I miss?"

Sarah began again. "I was saying Miriam's parents and older sister are here."

"Go on."

"Well, her mama is real bossy."

Silence. Finally Peggy spoke. "Mrs. Thompson hasn't seen her daughter in a year. Maybe that's her way of helping."

"Hmmm, it wasn't like that. She bossed everybody. She was giving Mr. Thompson orders like General Eisenhower gave his troops during the war. She took Eli from me, and gave him to Harriet."

"That's fine, honey. They've driven a long way to see and hold those babies."

"Poor Sadie was practically in tears because she was changing the supper menu. Aunt Miriam looked like she wanted the floor to open and swallow her, like Jonah's whale."

"They are a family, and used to each other's actions," reasoned the grandmother.

"When she took Eli away from me, she told me to go home."

Silence.

"She told you to *what?*"

"She told me to go home, so I did."

The bathroom door opened and the ladies of the house poured out. Papa Tom, at the bottom of the stairs looked up with alarm. He had been looking forward all afternoon to peace and quiet after a hectic day at the store.

"What's going on? Did someone yell *stampede?*"

Clara called over her shoulder, "Your supper will be on the table as soon as the biscuits get done. "You 'gotta eat fast, cause I got to straighten out some folks."

Sarah brushed past, followed by Granny Jewel.

"Stop, wait, whoa!" exclaimed the grandfather, taking his wife's arm. "What is going on here?"

"Someone has insulted your beautiful, sweet granddaughter."

He put his newspaper on the hall table, sure by the time he read it, the news would be cold. "Start at the beginning," he ordered.

When all were seated in, Sarah once again told her experience.

When she finished, Granny Jewel stated, "After supper, we're going to straighten out that dear lady."

"After supper, you'll do no such thing."

"Thomas, our granddaughter's honor is at stake. "No one is going to tell **my** grandchild to get out and go home!"

Sarah's eyes grew wide with alarm. "It's OK, Granny Jewel. She wasn't real, real hateful. She was giving orders like she always does, I guess."

"Slow down, Jewel, and finish your supper. The Civil War has been over for almost one hundred years, and we're not going to start it again." He laid his fork on the side of his desert dish. "Clara, would you come in here, please."

Clara advanced on the dining room, wooden stirring spoon in hand.

"I know Sarah is grateful each of you is ready to do battle for her. That's what families are supposed to do. However, we must keep peace. If you go to Herb's house and blast his mother-in-law, you'll come home feeling pleased with yourself. Where will that leave Herb? His love and loyalty now is to his wife and children, but he also reveres his mother, sister and niece. There's bound to be hard feelings." His eyes searched each face, settling on his wife's. "Honey, it will be you who will see our grandchildren take their first step, and say their first word. It's you they'll show where they lost their first tooth. You're the grandmother they'll run to when they skin their knees, or want a box of animal crackers. The other grandmother will be a thousand miles away."

No one spoke for several minutes. "Of course you're right, Tom. You're always right. We will plan a more subtle approach." The woman drained her coffee cup, and carefully placed it in the saucer. "You know, my grandmother used to tell me about the Yankee occupation during the Civil War. In the town where she lived, the people were polite, but distant. Even though the North was the victor, never could they conquer the spirit of the Southern people."

"Exactly."

Granny Jewel, eyes bright announced, "If our grandparents could do it, we can do it! Tomorrow we'll invite all to high tea!"

# Chapter 6

Joshua slowly opened his eyes the following morning and saw his grandfather standing beside the bed. One finger was pressed tightly against his lips. "What's the matter, Papa?" he whispered, sitting up in bed. "Are we trying not to wake up Granny Jewel? Are we going fishing?" Before his grandfather could answer, he continued. "Aren"t me and Mackie going to work at the store today?"

"Mackie and I," corrected the grandfather. "Get some clothes on, I'm taking you and Mackie to breakfast at Mathes' Café."

"Why, Papa? Is Clara sick? Where is Mama?" Joshua asked, alarmed.

"Your mama's fine, everybody's fine. I'll explain on the way."

Joshua dressed, was down the stairs and out the back door in a matter of seconds. He crawled through the fence where two palings were missing and hurried to Mackie's house. "Papa Tom is taking us to the café for breakfast," explained Joshua. Mackie, in pajamas, stood with his arms across his chest. His eyes barely open.

"What's going on? Clara fixes our breakfast on the days we work. Is she sick?"

Joshua was surprised at his friend's concern.

"No, Clara is fine. Papa Tom says he'll explain everything. He's waiting for us in the driveway so we have to hurry."

Joshua stepped through the hole in the fence and waited for Mackie. The older boy struggled to fit through the small opening. "I'm gonna bust another paling out of this fence before summer's over," he vowed. "I can't hardly fit anymore."

"It must be Clara's cooking," said Joshua, grinning.

When the three were safely away, Mackie asked, "What's going on, Mr. Mitchell? How come we ain't eating at your house?" His face brightened. "Are we hiding from the police?"

Tom Mitchell slowed his step and gazed overhead. "I'll explain in military terms: Joshua's grandmother is going to war this afternoon. Right now our women folks are preparing the battlefield. That is, they are cleaning, dusting and scrubbing every inch of the house. Sarah is polishing silver and ironing linens."

Mackie was intrigued. "What are they using for ammunition?"

"Let's see," said the grandfather, "homemade lemon cookies that melt in your mouth, cherry tarts in thin, flaky crusts, and sandwiches the size of a vanilla wafer. Hot tea will be poured from a silver tea pot and drunk from delicate china cups."

Mackie wiped perspiration from his forehead with the back of his hand. "You're not making sense, Mr. Mitchell."

"It's true, Mackie," added Joshua. "I heard them talking at supper last night. What they're planning to do is be nice to their enemies, like the Bible says to do."

"I got a better plan for *my* enemies," declared Mackie, closing one hand over a fist.

"Let's get a good table by the window where we can feel the breeze," suggested Papa Tom before Mackie could elaborate on the fate of his enemies.

"I got one more question," said Mackie, looking over the top of the breakfast menu, "What are they using for weapons?"

"Sharp wits and soft tongues."

"I'm sorry I asked," mumbled Mackie, studying the menu.

Before the meal was over, the front door of the café opened. And an older woman came in, surveyed the scene, and took a table near the door.

"I know her," said Mackie, rolling scrambled egg on his tongue. "She's a crabby old lady."

Papa Tom, curious turned, "Oh, that's Miss Sophie Garner. She's nice. What makes you say she's crabby?"

Mackie took a long drink of milk, wiped his lips with the back of his hand, and leaned closer to the grandfather. "It's like this. Last week when I was sweeping the sidewalk in front of the store, she came by. I thought it might be good for business to do a little advertising, like they do on the radio."

Papa Tom rolled his eyes. "What did you say to Miss Sophie?"

"I told her not to walk by, but come in and buy something. I said it real nice at first."

"What did she say, Mackie?" All of Papa Tom's attention was on the boy sitting beside him.

"She said she had been shopping at C.D. Jones grocery store for forty years and was not of a mind to change."

"Did you thank her very nicely and go about your work?"

"Not exactly."

"Tell me what you said next, Mackie."

"I told her she was a fool if she didn't shop at Mitchell's. She ignored me, so I yelled and told her we didn't want her damn business anyway."

Tom Mitchell quietly placed his fork on the side of the plate. "Oh, no, oh, no," he murmured.

"What's wrong, Mr. Mitchell? It don't hurt none to try and drum up a little business."

"Mackie, we need to have a talk, but this isn't the place. We need to get the store open and then we'll go in the office and discuss a right and a wrong way to advertise."

"I'm fired, ain't I?" questioned the boy, staring at his empty plate. "My daddy says there's all kinds of ways people tell you you're fired. Some say it nice, and some come right out and say, 'You're fired! Either way, you're out a job and broke." Mackie's eyes glistened with unshed tears.

"You're not fired, Mackie. You still have your job, but there's something you have to do."

"Sure, Mr. Mitchell! I'll do anything," Mackie replied. "My daddy says I better not lose this job or he'll beat my . . ."

"We get the picture, Mackie," interrupted the grandfather. "Now, when we leave, I want you to stop at Miss Sophia's table and apologize to her for your strong language."

Mackie slowly put his glass of milk on the table, forgetting to wipe the mustache from his upper lip. "You want me to do *what*?"

"You heard me, Mackie," said Papa Tom sternly.

The boy's jaw was firmly set, his eyes mere slits. "I ain't saying nothing to that old biddy."

Joshua, entranced by the whole conversation, knew neither would back down. "Mackie, do you like it when people try to tell you what to do?"

"Nobody tells me what to do." Mackie's eyes were tiny slits, his lower lip sticking out.

"I'll bet Miss Sophie is the same way," Joshua hurried on. "She might be a real nice lady if you don't try to tell her what to do. She lives by herself so she doesn't have anybody to protect her or take up for her. I guess she has to be tough to survive."

Mackie leaned over and peeped around Papa Tom. He saw a little lady with gray hair in a tiny knot on the back of her head. Her shoulders were stooped, like she was carrying a heavy load. "She don't look so big sittin' down."

"She's really a very nice lady," added Papa Tom, picking up the bill. "I'm going to pay and walk out the door. I know you'll do the right thing. When you finish, come over and get to work. We've got a lot to do today, and we need to get busy."

Joshua moved to follow his grandfather. He suddenly felt an iron grip on his wrist. "Don't go, Joshua. I can't face that old bid . . ., I mean, that nice lady by myself. I need you to do the talking."

"Oh, no, Mackie! I'm not going to do the talking. But, I'll stand by you while you apologize."

The older boy stood, clasping and unclasping his fist. For the first time, Joshua saw fear on his friend's face. "You know what, Mackie, her mama's dead, too. I'll bet she thinks about her a lot and misses her."

"Yeah," the boy said slowly. "I know what that feels like."

The distance from their table to hers, was agonizingly long. As they approached, Miss Sophie looked up. She instantly recognized the boy standing before her. She slowly lowered her coffee cup and waited.

"Lady," squeaked Mackie, his voice unnaturally high, "Mr. Mitchell told me I'm sorry for talking bad to you the other day." Perspiration stood on the boy's forehead, threatening to course down his face.

A smile slowly spread across the lady's face. "What's your name, young man?"

"Mackie Fuller. My daddy's Mack Fuller and he works at the hardware store. My mama's dead."

"So is mine, Mackie."

Unbidden, he slipped into the chair across from Miss Sophie. "Do you miss her worse at night, and think of things you want to tell her?"

Miss Sophie leaned forward. "I do, Mackie. I really do. I don't think you ever get too old to miss your mama."

"I get real lonesome after school until daddy gets off work."

"I know. My house gets mighty quiet sometimes. I guess you could pass the time doing homework."

"I ain't that lonesome."

The waitress appeared. "Will that be everything, Ma'am?"

Miss Sophie smiled, "How would you boys like a cinnamon bun? I do hate to eat alone."

"No, thanks, Miss Sophie," Joshua said. "I'm going over and help Papa open the store." He turned to leave, realizing they hadn't heard.

"I guess I could choke one down," replied Mackie, smiling at the thought of melted icing running over the ridges of the warm pastry.

Papa Tom looked up as his grandson came in the store. "I was beginning to worry, Son. I see Mackie's not with you. I guess he decided to go home." Papa Tom looked discouraged.

"No sir. They're eating a cinnamon bun, and talking about all kinds of things. They didn't know I was there, so I left."

Later, polishing a bin of apples in front of the store, the grandfather saw Miss Sophie being carefully helped across the street. *That lady's spry as a cricket,* he thought. *She doesn't need help any more than I do.*

"Tom Mitchell," she said, when they reached the store, "you have yourself one fine young gentleman working for you. I'm liable to stop in from time to time. providing, of course, Mackie is here to wait on me."

'Thank you Miss Sophie. Yes, sir, Mackie is a treasure. We're mighty lucky to have him."

After the boys dusted the shelves and swept the floor, Mackie turned to Papa Tom. "What was it you wanted to talk to me about, Mr. Mitchell?"

"Never mind, Mackie. I think you could teach me a thing or two."

Lunch was a can of tiny sausages, saltines and a bottle of Coca-Cola. "Now, men, I have to send you on a rescue mission," announced Papa Tom. Mackie paused, a sausage half way his lips. "Think of Miriam's father as a prisoner of war. If we don't rescue him, he will be forced to attend high tea at my house. The man hasn't done anything bad enough to have to attend high tea. I want you to go around to Aunt Miriam's and announce that we are going fishing after lunch, and want him to come along."

Uncle Herb, sitting on a sack of flour, added, "Don't let him look at his wife for permission, or he's a gonner. Just tell him to meet us at the store at one o'clock. Tell him Daddy *needs* him."

Papa Tom looked at his son. "Aren't you stretching the truth a little?"

"No, Daddy. You might need Ralph to help you uh, uh, count fish."

"That sounds like a fish story to me, and we haven't even left the dock!"

A half hour later, Joshua returned to the grocery store. "How did it go?" asked Uncle Herb after he finished waiting on a customer.

Joshua rolled his eyes, "Boy, you should have heard Mackie! Lies were rolling off his tongue like water."

"Daddy's in the office. He'll want to hear this."

With the door discreetly closed, Joshua led into his story. "Well, first off, we had to go through introductions, then say something nice about the twins. I mostly covered for Mackie cause he looked so uncomfortable. When things got quiet, he started. He told a story about his daddy attending high teas. He said his daddy was a big man, and one time when he was holding a fine china cup, he accidently bit a hole in it. Another time, he couldn't get his big finger through the handle, and dropped it on the floor. While he was trying to kick the pieces under the table, he missed and kicked the table, and the silver tea pot fell off. Another time he ate too many cherry tarts with flaky crusts and got sick and had to barf in the lady's bathroom. Then the best part of all," said Joshua, holding his sides. "He said his daddy sometimes gets real windy after a big lunch, and by four o'clock . . ."

"What happened then?" asked Uncle Herb, wiping tears with his apron.

"Mrs. Thompson wouldn't let Mackie finish talking. She told us we needed to leave, so Mackie said we'd leave if Mr. Thompson could be excused from the high tea, and go fishing instead."

"What did she say?" asked Papa Tom, grinning.

"She was so busy herding us out the front door, I'm not sure what she said."

At exactly one o'clock, the door of Mitchell's grocery store opened. A tall, thin gentleman with graying hair stepped inside. Cautiously, he peeped outside, looking in the direction from which he had come. "Hello, Ralph," said Papa Tom, holding out his hand.

"It's nice to be here, Tom. I don't mind saying I'm *very* glad to be here. The lads saved me from a long, painful afternoon." He thought a minute. "Of course, I don't mean it would be painful to visit in your home."

Papa Tom slapped him gently on the back. "Painful is the right word, Ralph. That's why we're staying as far away as possible."

Ralph Thompson looked around the store. "Where is the other lad?"

"Mackie had to help his father this afternoon," said Joshua.

"I don't suppose they're invited to someone's house for tea?"

Papa Tom untied his white apron. "No, Ralph. There's very little chance of that."

Armed with a bucket of sand fiddlers, fishing lines, cookies and sodas, the three hurried to the dock were Papa Tom's thirteen foot row boat was tied. Ralph had been outfitted in sneakers, and a straw hat. "We're going to use the oars today, Ralph, because my outboard motor made strange sounds the last time we went fishing."

"This might be better, Tom. Now we can sneak up on the fish."

"Hmmm, I never thought of that," said Papa Tom, winking broadly at his grandson.

The afternoon breeze sent ripples across the clear blue-green water. On the far shore, outer banks ponies, their heads down, could be seen grazing in the marsh grass. An occasional sailboat whispered past, slicing the water at a rakish angle. The New Yorker sitting in the stern, twisted and turned, marveling at the beautiful scene. Along the edge of a narrow shallow, pelicans and cormorants were sitting, waiting for the incoming tide which would bring lunch.

"Tom," said Ralph, whispering, "This is paradise on earth. I'm so glad my grandchildren will be growing up here. I wish I lived here, too."

"You can do like Joseph when he was governor of Egypt" offered Joshua. "He sent for his whole family to come and live in the land of Goshen. You could bring your whole family down here."

"It might not be easy, Joshua, but I'll think about it. And this winter, when the snow is knee deep, I'll dream about today."

Tide, rushing in First Deep Creek, brought fish from Beaufort Inlet. The little skiff was anchored near a secret fishing hole, discovered the summer before.

Ralph, whose face and arms were already turning pink, concentrated on the art of baiting a hook, and getting it overboard. Soon, there was a jerk and a tug on the man's line. He stood, and in a rich baritone, announced, "I've got one. I caught a fish!" Rapidly he pulled in the line and brought a fine gray trout over the side.

"Wow!" exclaimed Joshua. "He's frying size!"

By six o'clock, the fishermen were weary, hungry, and ready to head home. There was a bucket of nice size fish, but none as fine as Ralph's trout.

"I wish we had a camera. Nobody back home will believe I caught a fish that big."

"What are you going to do with him, Mr. Thompson?"

"I suppose you can have him for your supper, Joshua. Ruth doesn't like seafood."

"We'll take the fish home and clean them. Then I'll send Joshua around with a plate full of filleted fish. Ask Sadie to fry them crisp and brown for your breakfast. With a cup of hot coffee and a pan of her fluffy biscuits with a golden crust and melted butter inside, you'll have a meal fit for a king. Oh, and by the way, don't use a fork. Eat the little fish with your hands. They taste better."

Ralph nodded slowly, then frowned. "Ruth doesn't like the smell of fried fish in her kitchen."

"It isn't *her* kitchen."

High Tea was history. The combatants were stretched across the furniture in the living room, too tired to talk. Amy was sleeping peacefully in her mother's lap, when the fishermen stepped in the back door. Granny Jewel raised one hand and pointed to the bathroom. "Bath," she said, "I smelled you before I saw you. Go!"

Papa Tom turned to his fishing partner. "You take your bath, and I'll deliver the fish to Sadie."

Joshua smiled and shook his head. "No, no, Papa. You said **I** was going to take the fish. I'll take my bath after you."

When Joshua returned, there was clam chowder and corn meal hush puppies on the table. "No one has the strength to cook," announced Granny Jewel.

"Well, ladies, how was your afternoon? Please don't leave out a single detail," said Papa Tom. "Joshua and I want to hear all about it."

"Thomas," said Granny Jewel, smiling triumphantly, 'if it had been a ball game, the score would be seven to nothing in our favor. I will admit, though, Ruth got in a few hits. First, she thought our ceilings too high. She said the house would be hard to heat in a snow storm. I told her it snows in Beaufort on the average of once every six years, and seldom covers autumn leaves."

"We told her she was lucky to have lovely, white snow, especially at Christmas," added Peggy. "When she hinted that our furniture looked a bit worn, I told her in the south, we're proud of furniture that has been in the family for generations. Old pieces that belonged to ancestors have a rightful place in our families."

"She scoffed at that, and said now that the girls were grown, they had all new furniture," added Sarah. You won't believe what Granny Jewel said then."

Papa Tom rolled his eyes. "Try me."

"My grandmother picked up a china cup and began pouring tea from the silver tea pot. She smiled at Mrs. Thompson and said, 'Aren't you fortunate. Our children beg to have their name put on the bottom of a favorite piece of furniture.' She handed the cup to her and murmured, 'You won't have to worry about that.'"

"The twins started getting fretful, and had to be fed, so the rest of the time we talked about them," added Granny Jewel.

"Oh, Papa," laughed Sarah, trying not to choke, "you should have seen Clara! She showed up at three forty-five in that black dress that's two sizes too small. She had washed and starched her white ruffled apron and maid's cap. Every time Granny Jewel or Mama asked her something, she'd say, "Yas'm, Miz Jewel, or, No'm, Miz Jewel. When Granny wasn't speaking in her soft, cultured voice, she was shooting daggers at Clara with her eyes."

"The best part," added Peggy, giggling, "was Mama trying to introduce Clara to Mrs. Thompson and her daughter. Clara got a sorrowful look on her face and said, "I iz jest the hired help, Ma'am. I know my place and it's in the kitchen." Then, she turned and swayed slowly out of the room. I've never seen Mama brave enough to be mad at Clara, but she was today."

"You mentioned the daughter. What's she like?" All three spoke at once.

"Wait! You first, Jewel."

"Oh, Thomas, what a marvelous project she would be! The girl is very beautiful in a quiet way. She wears her hair in an old timey bun on the back of her neck, and dresses like someone sixty years old. She even had on stockings and heavy shoes in this heat!

"She hardly said a word, Daddy. When we asked her a question, she would start to answer, and her mother would butt in and answer for her."

"But, Papa Tom," said Sarah when she could get in a word, "you should see her when she's holding one of the babies. Her smile is so sweet, and it lights up her whole face. She's really beautiful."

"Why do I sense a plan forming in those pretty heads?"

"Why, when have I ever interfered in the life of another?" asked Granny Jewel.

All quickly looked down and sipped another spoonful of delicious, thick, clam chowder.

# Chapter 7

"Mackie Fuller, what are you doing hanging around the back door on the Fourth of July? You know Mr. Mitchell's not going to open the grocery store today. It's a holiday, and everybody's having a picnic."

Mackie's face was pressed against the screen, his nose flat. "I know that, Clara, but I have to check on something." The boy eased the screen door open and put one foot hesitantly on the kitchen floor.

"Every fly in Beaufort is going to think that open door is an invitation to come in and have breakfast with the Mitchell's," declared Clara.

Mackie took this as an invitation to step inside the sparkling clean room which always held his nose captive with fragrant aromas. His eyes rested on a three layer chocolate cake Clara was busily icing. He watched the movement of the broad knife blade as it carried swirls of shiny gooey chocolate from a bowl to the still warm layers.

"I came over to see if you had any of that stuff left over from yesterday. I could help you get rid of it, if it's in the way." offered Mackie. "Besides, I want to see a sandwich the size of a vanilla wafer."

"Who told you about the sandwiches?"

"Mr. Mitchell told me and Joshua. I want to see if he was lying."

81

"Not only are they real, they don't have a top. They're called open-faced sandwiches, and they're the size of a slice of cucumber."

"Cucumber sandwiches! Yuck, that sounds awful!" Mackie grabbed his throat and rolled his eyes. "Cucumbers are what you *don't* put on a salad."

"I suppose you'd like to test a cherry tart . . ."

"A cherry tart with a light flaky crust?" interrupted Mackie, grinning. "How about throwing in a few lemon cookies, guaranteed to melt in your mouth?"

"Pull that stool up to the counter. It so happens I saved the leftovers for just such an occasion." From the refrigerator, Clara took a glass tray covered in wax paper. She carefully slid the stand holding the chocolate cake aside and made room for the tray. When she removed the paper, Mackie could only gasp.

"Whoa, Nellie!" He exclaimed, his eyes raking the array of dainty pastries.

"Help yourself, Boy. This stuff will get soggy if somebody doesn't eat it." Clara put a plate before Mackie and continued icing the magnificent chocolate sculpture. Mackie, feasting on the dainty food, watched in fascination as Clara swirled the icing, leaving it in tiny peaks. She smiled as she watched the boy tenderly remove each dainty pastry and pop it in his mouth.

"M-m-m-m," he moaned with each bite.

"I believe you'd clean the tray, if I let you." She wrapped the remainder of the food in several layers of wax paper. "Take this to your daddy. I'll bet he'd enjoy a cherry tart."

"With thin, flaky crust," added Mackie, licking his fingers.

"Go on with you, now. Mr. James Bowers will be getting here from Raleigh by noon time, and I aim to see he gets a meal he won't soon forget."

As Mackie turned to leave, Joshua stuck his head around the door. "Mackie!" he exclaimed, surprised. "I didn't know you were here. Why didn't you wake me?"

"He didn't come over here to see you," said Clara, standing back and surveying her chocolate masterpiece. "He came to help me dispose of leftovers."

Joshua followed his friend. Already a broad shaft of sunlight on the porch was hot enough to burn bare feet, promising another blistering day. "What are you going to do now, Mackie?"

The boy, holding tightly to his tray of indescribable treasures, looked at Joshua. "Us older boys swim off the government dock every Fourth of July."

"What's so special about the Fourth of July?"

"Don't you know nothin'? I swear, I have to tell you everything."

"I don't live here all the time, remember," Joshua said defensively. "Tell me, what's so special about going swimming today?"

Mackie took a deep breath and glanced at his friend. "Today's the day you have to get mud. If you can't get mud, you're a sissy pants. The tough guys won't have anything to do with you."

Joshua slapped at a mosquito singing in his ear. What's so hard about getting mud? There's plenty of it on the shore at low tide."

"*From the deepest part of Taylor's Creek?*"

"Huh?"

"That's right. You have to dive down in the deepest part of the channel, bring up a handful of mud, and hold it up for everybody to see."

"I can do that."

Mackie's boisterous laughter filled the air. He slapped his pal on the back. "The only way you could get mud out of the channel is to hire a dredge."

Joshua stood, his fists clenched, and glared at the older boy. "I can swim as good as you."

"What makes you think so?" asked Mackie, irritated.

"Because, I take lessons at the YMCA in Raleigh during the winter."

Mackie laughed again. "Paddling around in a heated swimming pool with a lifeguard is a little different from swimming in muddy sea water and dodging fishing boats that could cut you up in little pieces." Mackie put his hand on his friends shoulder. "Hey, don't worry about it. Nobody expects you to get mud. You're kinda' puny, and you're an upstater."

"You don't have to make excuses for me," said Joshua angrily. "I'll be down there after awhile, and I'll show all of you."

"Joshua," called a voice from inside.

Mackie strolled toward the opening in the fence, turned and yelled, "Your mama's calling you, kid. Better hurry inside."

Joshua stormed in the house, almost knocking his mother down. "What?"

He glared at the person he loved most. "What do you want?"

"Young man, what do you mean, 'What do I want?' You march yourself to the table, and I'll be expecting an apology!"

"I'm not apologizing, cause I haven't done anything wrong."

"Now you are contradicting me, besides being disrespectful." Peggy rose to her full five feet three inches, and pointed upstairs. "Go to your room and don't come out until you are ready to apologize."

Joshua stomped up the steps, slammed his bedroom door, and threw himself across the bed. "Everybody hates me," he mumbled, directing his words at a tiny crack in the ceiling. "It would serve them right if I swam out to the middle of the creek and drowned." Joshua imagined the police coming to the door and telling the sad news to his family. *Mama would be sorry she treated me so mean,* he thought. *Sarah would cry for days and wish she'd been nicer to me. My grandparents . . .*" He suddenly sat up in bed, wiped a tear, and rested his chin on his hands. "My grandparents' hearts would break," he said aloud. Tears began to fall faster. Furiously he wiped them away with the back of his hand and started to the door.

Downstairs the family was eating breakfast. His mother's voice rose above the others. "I can't imagine what got into that boy. He has never sassed me like that."

Joshua quietly tiptoed down the steps, avoiding the one that squeaked. "Peggy, it's all part of growing up. I'm sure he didn't mean to be disrespectful," answered her father.

"Mackie may have said something that upset him," added Sarah. It made him feel better to hear his sister's defense.

"Mama," he said, appearing in the doorway, "I'm sorry for what I said. Can I come out of my room now?"

"I accept your apology, Son. Now come to the table and eat your breakfast, although it's probably cold. I'll ask Clara to serve you another plate."

"No, no, Mama. I'm not really hungry." It was true. The boy had more on his mind than scrambled eggs and toast. He looked at his mother imploringly. "Can I go swimming with Mackie?"

His mother was silent for a minute. "Do you think it's safe, Daddy?"

Papa Tom stared at his grandson. "Do you promise to be careful, and not do anything dangerous? I know things can get out of hand when there's a group of boys."

"We can all go when your father gets here," suggested his mother. "He might like a cool swim after driving in the heat."

Joshua felt panic rise in his throat. How would it look to the fellows on the government dock if he was swimming with his *family*! Anger flared his nostrils. "Nobody else has to have their mama watch them. How old do I have to be before I can swim with the other boys?" No one answered, so he continued, "When Sarah was twelve, she was allowed to go places without her parents."

"You're only eleven."

He looked at his grandfather. "Yes, but boys are stronger than girls, and can do more things."

"I'm thinking of one thing I can do, and that's bop you on the head," said his older sister, glaring at him over a bowl of grits.

"Let's compromise," said his mother brightly. "Suppose Sarah goes with you instead of your parents?"

Joshua hit his forehead with the palm of his hand. "I'd rather be shot at sunrise than to show up with my big sister."

"There was never a problem with Sarah having to prove herself," moaned Peggy.

"Boys are different, Honey," said her father over a second cup of coffee. "There are rites of passage into young manhood. We don't want him branded a sissy. It would be a hard reputation to live down."

"Joshua," said his mother, looking him in the eye "you may go swimming with Mackie and the boys. Be careful, and be home by lunch time." The mother rolled her eyes. "I'll not breathe easy until you're back in this house."

"He's growing up, honey," said Granny Jewel. "You have to trust him."

"It's a wonder my hair isn't snow white. Strange boys show up here to date my daughter, and my son prefers being with a gang of boys, instead of his family.

"I'm thankful Amy is only four years old, and loves to be with her mama."

"I want to go to Laney's house," announced Amy.

Joshua, fearful his mother would change her mind, took the steps two at a time. In a matter of seconds, he was in his swim trunks and back downstairs. "I'll be back soon," he called, leaping off the front porch. He was still running when he turned the corner. *I'm safe now*, he decided. *Mama can't change her mind and call me back.*

He could see Taylor's Creek as he neared Front Street. The water sparkled as a cool breeze rippled the surface. Suddenly, it didn't look inviting. Joshua slowed his step. *Suppose something happens and I don't get home for lunch or ever again? Suppose I come up empty handed if front of all the boys?*

"Here he comes, guys. Didn't I tell you he'd show up?" Mackie seemed relieved to see his friend, and pulled him aside. "I knew you'd come, because you never go back on your word. Now listen," Mackie moved closer and whispered, "Take three or four deep breaths before you go under. That will help you hold more air. The deeper you go, the darker it gets. When you get to the bottom, grab a big handful of mud and hold it in your fist so it won't wash out. Push off the bottom with both feet so you will get to the surface faster. By then you'll feel like your lungs are gonna' bust."

As his friend talked, Joshua's knees began to feel weak. Fearing his legs would no longer hold him, he turned and walked toward the end of the dock, realizing Mackie was now wearing a worried expression. The older boy glanced at the group and then looked at Joshua. Suddenly he leaned down, his nose dangerously close. "Now don't you go and get yourself hurt." Glancing behind to be sure the other boys were still talking among themselves, Mackie whispered. "If you get in trouble I'll come in after you."

Mackie swiftly straightened and took a step backward as the other boys moved closer. A sea of grinning faces swam before his eyes. "Come on, kid. We got a bet you can't get mud."

"You're not strong enough," taunted another. The boys moved aside, clearing the end of the dock. Joshua stood for a moment, looking down at the blue-green water.

"What's the matter, kid, are you waiting for your mama to hold your hand?"

This comment was greeted with laughter.

Joshua, his throat dry, turned, "I don't see any mud in your hands. Maybe none of you can get mud."

"We already did, now it's *your* turn."

In one sudden movement, Joshua jumped off the end of the dock. He broke the surface of the water with a splash, cool salt water closing over his head. He surfaced, and without looking back, began swimming toward the middle of the channel. "Oh, God, be not far from me," he whispered, having heard his sister use this scripture from the Bible.

When he reached the middle of the channel he turned, treading water to stay afloat. The boys on the dock seemed far away. Cars passed on the street, and people strolled along the sidewalk. Suddenly, the boy felt completely alone. For the first time, there was no parent or big sister to protect him. He started to take a deep breath, and choked on a mouthful of salt water. Spitting it out, he took several deep breaths as Mackie instructed. On the fourth, he plunged beneath the surface. He was surprised there was no sound, only a silent green world. Kicking furiously, he swam downward into the dark, murky world fifteen feet below the surface. As he continued forcing his way to the bottom, it became too dark to see. Finally, his right hand touched something. It was cool, soft, **mud**!

Frantically, he sunk his hands in the grainy substance, and with both fists clenched, pushed with all his strength against the sandy floor of the channel. His body shot toward the surface but made little headway with both fists closed.

Joshua felt a hot pain in his chest, and feared he would never make it to the surface where there was fresh, cool air. Legs weak, he struggled toward the distant glow, fighting the desire to inhale, knowing to do so would be his end. He opened his left hand and shaped it like a cup in order to pull more water. The mud, so carefully gathered, disappeared below. Now, the surface loomed closer. With another thrust of his left arm and legs kicking, he broke the surface of the water. A wailing sound escaped his throat as air rushed to his starved lungs. He gasped for breath, the burning in his chest gone. *I did it*, he thought. *I did it! I got mud! Even if it's all gone, I don't care! My life's worth more than a handful of mud. If nobody believes me, I'll always know I did it.*

"Hold up your hand," someone yelled. He turned and faced the group far away on the dock. Treading water, he held his arm high and opened his right fist. Something cool slid down his arm. Before he could focus, a cheer went up from the group. Wiping salt water from his burning eyes, he saw gooey, gorgeous black mud stuck in the palm of his hand.

Slowly, he swam toward the dock, his breath still coming in gasps. When he reached the ladder, willing hands yanked him from the water and dropped him on the dock. He closed his eyes and lay against the warm, solid planks.

"That was real good, Joshua," said one of the older boys. Joshua smiled. He was no longer, 'kid' or 'boy', he was Joshua, who got mud in Taylor's Creek on the Fourth of July, 1949.

"Say, you want to hang around with us?" asked one of the older boys.

Joshua felt the thrill of being accepted. However, he remembered his mother's words. "Yeah, but my dad's coming today, and I haven't seen him all summer." Not for any amount of money would he tell his mother wanted him home in time for lunch.

A familiar car was in the driveway as Joshua rounded the corner. "Daddy's here!" he exclaimed. Bare feet slapping against the sidewalk, he hurried in the house. "Dad?"

"I'm in here, Son. Come give your father a hug." James Bowers, enjoying a glass of lemonade, stood when his son entered the room.

Joshua walked across the room and extended his hand. "What, no hug from my only son?"

"Dad, don't you think I'm a little too old for that sort of thing?"

The father, surprised, stammered, "Uh, well, I guess you're right. You're not a little boy anymore." James Bowers realized his son had not called him 'daddy.'

The father's words pleased Joshua. *It's true*, he thought. *I'm as tall as Mama, and almost as tall as Sarah. I hang out with boys older than I, and I can get mud.*

"Your mother told me you went swimming with the guys," said James returning to a chair by the window. "It must have felt different going without family."

"Yeah, Dad, it was real different. In fact, it was breathtaking."

The auditorium filled rapidly. Heavy dark green drapes at each tall window were pulled back and fastened, allowing every puff of cool air to find its way inside. A line all the way to the street formed quickly as each person waited patiently to pay their dollar. Nettie Blackwell and Harriet Thompson stood together. "It was so nice of you to invite me, Miss Blackwell," said Harriet.

"Oh, Child," the older woman said, patting Harriet's hand, "It always feels good to get out of the house for the evening." Before Miss Nettie could continue, someone in line turned and smiled at the two.

"Hi, Miss Nettie," she said cheerfully. "How are you?"

"Quite well, dear, and how are you?" These greetings continued until they were seated.

"Miss Blackwell, you are known by everyone in Beaufort, are you not?" Harriet could not keep amazement from her voice.

"Harriet, honey, I taught at least half the people in this auditorium, and I know the other half. That's what comes from teaching school in a small town."

"That is a wonderful legacy," replied Harriet.

The older woman smiled. "It's a darn sight better than receiving a gold watch after thirty years of faithful service and then put out to pasture." Across the aisle, the Bowers family was busy finding seats. Miss Nettie noticed Amy was with them. She leaned toward Harriet. "That child will likely squirm a hole in the seat before the performance is over."

"It's close to her bedtime. Maybe she'll curl up in her mother's lap and sleep through most of it," added Harriet. The ladies were entertained the next thirty minutes watching townspeople pour in. Miss Nettie described in detail the people as they hurriedly found seats.

As the heavy, dark green curtain rose, Harriet turned to her companion. "I feel I have lived in Beaufort most of my life."

Miss Nettie glanced at her new friend. "Perhaps you should consider living the rest of it here." Applause made any answer impossible.

The stage was decorated in red, white and blue crepe paper streamers. The chorus stood on risers against the back wall. Virginia Hassell, standing beside the piano, brought her hand down and forty voices burst into the song, "It's A Grand Old Flag." When the last note finished, a thunderous applause followed. Before the next selection, the audience was asked, by Mrs. Hassell, to stand for the Pledge of Allegiance. Footlights and a spotlight in the balcony illuminated all on stage. Granny Jewel, on the second row, looked more like Sarah's mother. Both were wearing bright make up and wore their hair swept back in matching gold clasps.

When Earl Willis strutted across stage in red and white striped pants and a star studded coat singing 'Yankee Doodle Dandy,' the audience roared, some coming to their feet. Near the close, all were asked to sing 'God Bless America.' Children, weary, leaned heavily on their parents. Adults, remembering the war, felt a stirring of patriotism. Veterans, close to tears.

Before closing the program with the National Anthem, Mrs. Hassell asked Nancy to step forward. The president of the senior class presented her with a dozen long-stemmed red roses which she graciously accepted. Her usual pale cheeks matched the beautiful flowers.

After several curtain calls, the chorus stepped down from the risers. "Hey, Tom," asked John Bell, "Who do you suppose the lady was sitting with Miss Nettie? I've never seen her before."

"She's Miriam's sister from New York." They moved slowly toward the steps.

"Is she married, and will she be here long?"

Tom Mitchell grinned. "The answer to both questions is, "no.""

"I'd like to meet her, and maybe get to know her better. Will you introduce me?"

"Sure, but, my friend, you'd better work fast. She and her parents are leaving in a few days."

"We'll have to see about that," said John Bell, looking determined.

# Chapter 8

"Hold up a minute, ladies, if you please," called Tom Mitchell. Dragging John Bell by the sleeve, he made his way through the people. They had to pause as people complimented them on their performance. "Thank you for waiting," he said to Miss Nettie, as they stepped from the crowd.

"Of course, Tom. I'm glad for an opportunity to tell both of you how much I enjoyed the evening." She turned to Harriet. "Don't you agree?"

The young woman had taken her characteristic stance behind whoever was talking. "Uh, yes, Mr. Mitchell. The performance was remarkable."

Tom Mitchell looked around Miss Nettie. "Harriet, I have someone here I'd like you to meet." He turned to his friend only to find he had stepped into the shadows. Papa Tom grabbed him by the sleeve once more and pulled him forward. Miss Nettie, watching the struggle, stepped aside and suddenly the two were face to face. After introductions, the two older people continued their conversation. Harriet stood clutching her purse and studying the toe of her brown oxford shoes. John Bell, jingling change in his pocket, studied constellations.

"You know what, Tom? I believe I dropped my lace handkerchief in the auditorium. It was rather warm, and I remember taking it out of my pocket. I wonder if you'd be a lamb, and help me look for it before they lock the building."

Papa Tom extended his elbow and Nettie Blackwell slid her arm through his as they hurried toward the building. Both looked where Miss Nettie and Harriet had been sitting. Suddenly, she exclaimed, "Oh, silly me! I looked in my purse again, and here's my handkerchief. It's been here all along."

"Miss Nettie," said Papa Tom, giving her a sly look, "if I didn't know better, I'd think you planned this." He was rewarded with a sly grin.

Under the street light, the strangers waited, silence a wall between them. When John saw his friends coming out of the school, he blurted, "Miss Harriet, I saw you sitting in the audience this evening, and I conspired to make your acquaintance. I hope you don't think that is too forward of me." His straw hat, clutched in his fist, quivered.

Harriet Thompson, with all the courage she could muster, answered, "Why, no, John." She paused and looked up. "Do you mind if I call you John?"

Hands shaking, John Bell quickly answered, "Oh, no, Miss Harriet. It would please me to no end if you'd address me by my given name."

"You don't have to call me 'Miss Harriet,'" she said, smiling.

John Bell took a step closer to the lovely young lady. "'Uh, Harriet, I wonder if I might call on you tomorrow evening." He rushed on. "I don't mean to seem forward, but Tom tells me you'll only be in Beaufort a few more days."

Harriet, taken with this man who spoke so courtly, replied, "Why, yes, John. I would be pleased if you called at my sister's house on Moore

Street." Suddenly, she didn't want to take a chance on this fine man not being able to find her.

"I know exactly the house, and I'll arrive soon after the drug store closes."

Harriet asked, "Do you work in a drug store?"

John Bell answered modestly. "Yes, I work there, but I also own the store."

Harriet brightened, turning her full smile on the defenseless bachelor. "I am a pharmacist, John. I work in a small drug store in my home town."

Before he could answer, the others walked up. "Come on, John. I'll drop you off at your house. My gang is waiting for me to take them to the Dixie Dairy for ice cream."

"You're fortunate, Tom, to have such a big, loving family."

"Yes, John, I thank God every day for such a blessing."

The ladies rode home in silence, Harriet marveling at how traffic parted when Miss Nettie's car was recognized. It's much like the parting of the Red Sea, she decided. When they were safely in the driveway, Harriet made no move to get out. "Miss Nettie, please tell me about John Bell," she said in the darkness. The only illumination was a small porch light.

"John was one of my students, many years ago."

Harriet grinned. "Somehow I knew you were going to say that," the younger woman interrupted.

Miss Nettie sat, her hand resting on the steering wheel. "John was a sweet boy, and is a sweet man. He has a gentleness and refinement seldom seen in others. Why, if someone needs medicine after the store is closed, they have only to call John at home and he'll go down, open the store and fill the prescription."

"Why hasn't he ever married?"

"When the other young people started dating, John was so shy the girls found him boring. He told me while he was in college he took extra courses and 'studied his head off,' as he likes to say. There was no time for girls."

Harriet remembered being much the same way. "My daddy worked hard to send four girls to college, and I didn't feel I could waste a minute on parties and dates."

"People can get in a rut, you know, and when John came home, he went to work in the drug store. His father died a few years ago, and John took over the store and has been there ever since."

"Miss Nettie, John asked if he may call on me tomorrow night. He asked in such a gentlemanly way, there was no way I could refuse. In fact, I could almost feel my heart beat a little faster."

"Harriet Thompson, you are a treasure!" The older woman patted Harriet on the arm. "Other women see John as a stick-in-the-mud, and you see him as a courtly gentleman."

"I may not be a fortune teller, but I think under that quiet exterior, there is a fun loving, Christian gentleman who is gentle and kind." Harriet opened the car door and looked back at her friend. "And Miss Nettie, I plan to find out!"

Miss Nettie came around to the other side of the car. "Good for you, Harriet. Good night, and sleep well."

When she got to the middle of the street, Harriet stopped and turned. "I have no intention of sleeping one wink!"

In the gray dawn, Harriet heard one of the twins cry out. *I still can't tell them apart from their cries*, she realized. Slipping on a bathrobe, she padded barefoot down the wide upstairs hall and went into the nursery. Miriam was already diapering Eli. "I'm sorry he woke you, Harriet," she whispered.

"Sister, I was already awake. In fact, I don't think I slept all night."

The younger sister looked alarmed. "Is anything wrong?"

Before Harriet could answer, Emma awoke and began to whimper. The aunt scooped her up, and gave her a dry diaper. "Let's take them downstairs for their bottle. I don't want the whole house to wake for a while."

"You'd better stop acting mysterious, or I'll tell Mama."

Harriet's smile faded. "Please tell me you're kidding."

"Of course, but, I'll pull your pigtail if you don't soon tell me what's causing that happy grin."

For a few minutes, each was satisfied to listen to the twins contented sounds as they drank a bottle of warm milk. "Miriam, I met a very nice man at the concert last night." Harriet took a deep breath and studied Emma's face. "He asked if he could call on me tonight."

"Are you making this up?"

"Certainly not! Why does it seem so impossible for a man to show interest in me?"

"Shhh, Harriet. Please keep your voice down. It doesn't seem impossible, just, uh, *improbable*." Miriam held Eli and patted his back. She was soon rewarded with a healthy burp. "Are you going to tell me who this mysterious stranger is?"

"His name is John Bell, and he owns Bell's Drug Store."

"Oh, I have met John. He seems very nice, but very quiet. He doesn't have much, uh, hair."

"Oh, Sister, do you think at *my* age hair, or the lack of it, is going to make a difference?"

"He isn't very tall."

"So what! He's taller than I, and that's all that matters. Not everybody can be as tall as the lanky Mitchell men."

"What are you going to do about Mama? She's sure to disapprove."

Harriet looked thoughtful. "I'll worry about that when the time comes."

Emma and Eli, after their bottles, went back to sleep. The sisters continued rocking. Harriet's eyes widened. "I just thought of something! I haven't a thing to wear on a date! I certainly didn't bring anything for stepping out with a gentleman." Harriet gave an uncharacteristic giggle.

"How much money did you bring?"

"Before we left, I drew several hundred dollars from my savings."

"Wow! That should be enough for a complete wardrobe." Miriam got up and tiptoed to the telephone.

"Who are you calling at this hour?"

"'This hour' is time to get up. I hear Herb stirring and it sounds like Mama is already barking orders at Daddy. I'm calling in the experts."

Miriam looked at her beloved sister. She knew Harriet's hairstyle had been out of fashion for years. Her drab, sensible clothes were birthday and Christmas gifts from their parents. She shuddered as she thought of Harriet's clunky brown shoes and heavy duty stockings.

"Mother Jewel," she whispered in the telephone, "I need you in a great way. No, nobody is sick. We're all in good health. I need my dear brown mouse sister transformed into a shimmering butterfly." She paused and listened. "When? Tonight, Mother Jewel. I need it done before tonight." There was another long pause. "Did you drop the telephone, Mother Jewel?"

Two hours later, the Mitchell car was whizzing over the causeway between Beaufort and Morehead City. Jewel Mitchell was at the helm. Sarah sat in the middle, and Nettie Blackwell beside the window. Miriam, Peggy and Harriet sat in the back.

"It is so very kind of you to help me, everyone," said Harriet. "I hope it's not an imposition."

"Harriet, honey, I wouldn't miss this for the world. The first thing we have to concentrate on is shoes. You need at least one pair of leather sandals, some low heel white pumps, and of course, a pair of high heel black and white spectator pumps."

"Have you told your parents about stepping out this evening," asked Miss Nettie, smiling over her shoulder.

"Yes," snickered Harriet. "She was so busy tending to two babies, she didn't have time to comment."

"I called Emily at the Duchess beauty parlor. You have an appointment for a haircut and manicure at three o'clock."

Harriet sounded doubtful. "I don't know what to tell her."

'Emily will know. We'll have enough time to have lunch at a café and choose several new dresses."

"Several, Mrs. Mitchell?"

"Of course, Harriet. You can't wear the same dress every day."

With several shoe boxes in hand, the group returned to Beaufort and descended on Potter's Dress Shop on Front Street. Virginia Potter welcomed all with a smile. "Good morning ladies. What can I help you with today?" Her eyes rested on Granny Jewel, the person clearly in charge.

"Virginia, I'd like you to meet Harriet Thompson, sister to my new daughter, Miriam."

Harriet stepped forward timidly "Oh, Harriet!" exclaimed Virginia. "What lovely skin you have! With a complexion like that, we must find something in a soft pink." Color rose to the young woman's cheeks, making her skin more beautiful. The clerk whisked a dress from the rack and held it before the girl.

Harriet slowly shook her head. "Maybe something more sensible."

"Sensible my eye! You're going to try that dress on!"

Harriet smiled. "You're getting might bossy, little sister."

Miriam hugged her sister. "You bossed me when we were growing up. It's my turn now."

All waited patiently for Harriet to emerge from the dressing room. When she did, only a sigh was heard. The dress, made of polished cotton shone in the overhead lights. Iridescent buttons on the front of the scoop neck bodice looked like jewels. The full skirt, accentuating Harriet's tiny waist, swirled with every step. Standing in front of a three-way, full length mirror, Harriet stared at her reflection.

"This dress is too beautiful to be real," she murmured. "I'm afraid I might spill something on it"

Sarah remembered the summer she was twelve. She had tried on a gorgeous pink dress in this very store that was several sizes too big. *Before I go back to Raleigh, I'll come down and look at their fall clothes. I won't have any trouble filling them out now.*

"Virginia, more dresses! We can't have Harriet wearing a dress she has to worry about all evening," declared Granny Jewel.

Arms loaded with crisp, colorful dresses, Virginia marched to the dressing room, followed by Harriet, who by now had cast off her old shoes for a pair of white sandals. Granny Jewel slipped the old shoes in the empty shoebox, hopefully never to be seen again.

Trying on each dress, Harriet's severe hair style loosened. Tendrils coiled around her face and neck. When she smiled, her full lips framed even, white teeth. Nettie Blackwell marveled at the beautiful young woman emerging before their very eyes.

Four dresses won the heart of the young woman. "I'll take these, Virginia," said Harriet. Granny Jewel looked up in time to see her staring wistfully at the first dress she tried.

"Change that to five dresses," she said, adding the shimmering pink to the ones being folded and placed in brightly colored boxes.

"I really shouldn't, Mrs. Mitchell," Harriet said doubtfully.

"Hush, Child, this dress is my treat. I don't know when I've had so much fun."

Lunch was the blue plate special at Mathes' Café. "Let's keep an eye on the time, girls," said Granny Jewel, enjoying the role of leader. "I had to move heaven and earth to get a hair appointment on a Friday afternoon."

"How did you manage?" asked Peggy.

"Emily rearranged several schedules, and actually had a cancellation the last minute."

After introductions, Emily escorted Harriet to her booth, where the young woman was asked to sit in a leather chair, facing a huge mirror. Emily stood back and stared, hands on hips. The rest formed a half circle, watching Emily's expression. "Hmmm," the artisan hummed, ignoring the onlookers. Eyes followed, as Emily studied Harriet from different angles. "Your profile should be on a cameo pin, honey. Also, we have to do something to accentuate those high cheek bones." She spun Harriet's chair. "The first thing we're going to do is get rid of that coil on the nape of your neck." Emily sunk her manicured nails in Harriet's hair and began furiously removing pins. Sarah watched as they flew through the air toward the counter, some landing on the floor. No one made a move to pick them up, for fear of missing something. Silky, dark blonde hair, freed from the confines of pins and hair form, cascaded around her shoulders. "I knew it!" exclaimed the hair dresser. "Besides having a face with perfect bone structure, you have *thick, silky* hair with *natural curl!*"

Harriet, staring at her image, felt a tear roll down her cheek. "Oh, honey! Did I hurt your feelings? I didn't mean to!"

"No, no, Emily," said Harriet, taking Emily's hand. "It's just that nobody ever said such nice things before."

"Honey, when I get through with you, you're going to have to get used to compliments, cause they'll be coming thick and fast."

For the first time, Emily turned to the others. "Ladies, this is going to take a little time. Would you be more comfortable sitting in the reception area?"

Each slowly shook their head. "No, no."

"I'm fine."

"Don't worry about me."

Emily, forgetting her audience, put her full attention on the luxurious hair. With a pair of pointed, silver scissors, the beautician began cutting. Where her hair had been severely tucked in a coil, there were now layers of fluffy curls. Finally, her work done, Emily whipped the protective cape from Harriet's shoulders, and spun the chair. The transformation was complete. Before them was a radiant, confident young woman.

"Behold, ladies, the *new* Harriet Thompson!"

The new Harriet Thompson stepped out of the car in front of her sister's home. Both parents were sitting on the porch while the twins napped. "Thank you all, for a day I will never forget," she said hastily, never taking her eyes off her mother.

Both stood when their older daughter step from the car. "Well, Harriet," said Ruth Thompson, hands on her ample hips. "It seems you have made a day of it. What are you wearing, and, where are *your* clothes?"

Before Harriet could answer, her father, ignoring the mother, stepped off the porch and extended his hand. "Harriet, my dear, you are beautiful!" Still holding hands, they stepped inside the house.

Mrs. Thompson, angry at being ignored, turned to her younger daughter. "What is the meaning of this, Miriam? What have you done to your poor sister?"

Others watched helplessly as Miriam shrank before her mother's accusing gaze. "Mama, Harriet is going out tonight, and didn't have anything appropriate to wear."

"Harriet's clothes are suitable for any occasion. And, what have you done to her hair?" The woman paused, "Harriet is going where?"

Miriam stepped up on the porch, eye level with her mother. "That's right, Mother. Harriet has a date. A fine gentleman is coming to call on her tonight, and I pray you will use your best company manners."

Ruth Thompson seemed to puff up twice her size. "Well, I never!" she exclaimed, yanking open the screen door.

Miriam hurried down the steps and walked over to the car. "I want to apologize for my mother, she . . ."

"Don't worry for a minute, Miriam, honey," said Granny Jewel with a wave of her hand. "Go inside and protect your big sister, and call first thing tomorrow with a full report."

# Chapter 9

At five minutes before seven o'clock that evening, a light tap was heard on the front screen door. Harriet, ready for some thirty minutes, made herself walk slowly through the front hall.

"Good evening, John," she said holding the door. "Won't you come in?"

John Bell, wearing a light blue summer suit, white shirt and tie, stepped hesitantly into the hall. "Good evening to you, Miss, I mean, Harriet." He cleared his throat which suddenly felt dry. "I must say you look quiet different," he said, never taking his eyes from the lovely woman.

"Why, John, I don't know if that is a compliment. Do I look better, or worse?"

"Oh, Harriet, you look positively radiant," he assured her. "You were beautiful last night, too, but now you are even more beautiful, if that is possible." He shook his head. "I fear I'm making a mess of things."

Harriet smiled, aware of his discomfort. "Come into the living room and meet my parents." *Let's get this over*, she thought wryly. Ralph Thompson rose when they entered the room and extended his hand. Rose remained seated, a stiff smile painted on her face.

"Won't you sit down, John?" asked Ralph.

"Perhaps another time, Mr. Thompson. Harriet and I have dinner reservations, and cannot be late." The couple hastily said their farewells, and hurried toward the front door. Outside, they took a deep breath and began to relax.

"John, do you really have dinner reservations at Mathes' Café?" asked Harriet, glancing shyly at the man beside her.

"Of course, Harriet. I closed the store an hour early, and stopped in to tell Lillian Mathes I had a very special evening planned, and asked her to save a table for two." John smiled at the lovely woman at his side. "I knew she had a million questions, but I didn't have time to talk."

When the couple turned the corner, the south breeze tossed Harriet's curls. She tried to smooth the wayward locks with one hand. "Your hair looks fine, Harriet," assured her escort. "If you live on the coast, the wind keeps your hair flying, at least, that's what people tell me."

"It feels so different, John. For years I have tamed it with hair pins, but, no more, ever."

John held the restaurant door for his companion. At seven thirty, the dinner rush was over, and tables were empty. Several men sat at the counter sipping coffee. Lillian Mathes hurried over. "Your table is ready," she said after introductions, and led them to a small table at the rear of the restaurant. A wooden screen, painted with nautical scenes, had been placed near the table, affording the couple a bit of privacy. The table had been laid with a snow white cloth, and cloth napkins, instead of the usual oil cloth covering and paper napkins. In the center of the table a vase held a bouquet of brightly colored zinnias. Sitting near the window, they could hear water lapping against dock pilings. The faint cry of a black skimmer on the far shore could be heard as it searched for a meal of silver minnows.

Lillian approached the table, and, with a flourish, placed a menu before each. "Where is Carol? She was here when I stopped in."

"I decided to give her the night off. I'll be working in her place."

"I hope she's not sick."

"Oh, no, John. She looked tired, so I told her I'd close up."

The couple carefully studied the menu while Lillian waited. Finally, "I recommend the clam fritters, Miss Thompson, and, where are you from?"

"I'm from Binghamton, New York, Lillian."

"The clam fritters would be a wise choice, Harriet," offered John.

When she nodded, Lillian continued. "Would you like fried potatoes, cole slaw, and are you visiting someone in Beaufort?"

"Yes, potatoes and slaw are fine, and, my parents and I are here visiting my sister."

"Tea or coffee, and, who is your sister?" When Harriet answered, Lillian seemed satisfied to take the order to the kitchen.

"Harriet, I'm very sorry about the interrogation. I know Lillian meant no harm, but that's the way it is in a small town."

Lillian smiled at the man sitting across the table. "John, you don't need to apologize. I find it very charming. In a city, no one knows if you're new in town or have lived there forever. Here, it's almost as if the people are an extension of your family."

When the plates of sizzling food arrived, Lillian dimmed the restaurant lights and lit a candle in the center of the table. A radio in the kitchen played soft dinner music. Lillian adjusted the screen to afford the young couple more privacy. When the men at the counter finished their coffee, she ushered them out, locked the door, and turned the 'open' sign to 'closed.'

"John, the clam fritters are simply delicious."

"The clams were probably dug on the last low tide. That's one advantage of living in a coastal town, the seafood is only hours old."

"What was it like, growing up in Beaufort? I'm interested, since Emma and Eli will grow up here."

As John told of school adventures, playing marbles and going barefoot all summer, Harriet had an opportunity to study the face of the man across the table. She was already accustomed to the absence of hair, and concentrated on his blue eyes and quiet smile. *How can it be*, she wondered, *that I have known this man for only a number of hours, and yet, it seems we have been friends for years.*

"What are your hopes and dreams for the future?"

The woman was shocked to realize she had been studying John, not what he was saying.

"Well, John, I suppose I'll return home and work at Norwich Pharmacuticals until I retire. I've thought of moving out and getting a place of my own, but Mama always has some argument against it." She looked away. "I suppose my future will be pretty much like my past, and the present."

"I dream of having a place in the country. In fact, a few years ago, I bought five acres outside of town. It has a pond surrounded by pine and oak trees. On pretty Sunday afternoons, I drive out and walk around, listening to birds and watching turtles sun themselves. Sometimes it's nice to get away, and other times, I feel lonely. When I bought it, my hope was to build a big, two story house and fill it with children, dogs and cats."

"You forgot to mention a wife."

"That's the part that hasn't worked out."

"Hot apple pie with ice cream is a good way to top off a seafood supper," announced Lillian, returning.

"It sounds delicious, but I couldn't eat another bite," said Harriet shaking her head.

"Lillian, we'll take a rain check if that's all right. I promise we'll be back."

"John, I'm afraid you'll have to break that promise. The restaurant is closed tomorrow, and Daddy wants to go home on Monday." The evening, which had been so joyful, suddenly seemed filled with dread.

"There's time to make the nine o'clock movie. Would you like to go?"

"If you don't mind, I'd rather walk along the waterfront. I much prefer that to a noisy western movie."

They thanked Lillian and waited while she unlocked the front door and ushered them out. "It was so nice of her to help make our evening special," said Harriet, as they walked along peering in store windows.

"Harriet, Lillian enjoyed the status of being first with the news that the town's bachelor had a date with a beautiful woman."

After taking a few steps, John glanced at his companion. "The sidewalks are terribly uneven in some places." He cleared his throat and continued. "I think it might be safer if I held your hand." It seemed the most natural thing to place her hand in his for the remainder of the walk. At midnight, they stepped up on the porch. "This has been the loveliest evening I can remember," she murmured, glancing at the young man beside her.

"It has for me, too. I hate to see it end." Tenderly, he took her hand. "I would be honored if you would attend church with me tomorrow."

"I shouldn't, really. We're leaving the next day, and I have to pack, and I need to spend time with Miriam and her family."

"I understand, perfectly. My hope will be that we can correspond during the year." John turned to go. "Thank you again, Harriet, for a lovely evening." He stepped off the porch and began walking toward home.

Harriet, her hand on the doorknob, turned, and flew down the steps. "John, John," she called, not caring who might hear. John Bell stopped and turned. "I'll go to church with you. I'd love to go to church with you."

The dim light from the corner street lamp showed John's wide smile. "This is simply marvelous, Harriet. I will call for you at ten forty-five A.M."

Harriet waved good night and walked toward the house. *Yes,* she thought, almost skipping, *and I shall wear another new dress and new shoes, and curls.*

At breakfast, Harriet announced she would be going to church with John.

"Don't you think you're seeing too much of this man?" asked her mother, disapproving.

"No, Mother. I'm not seeing too much of John. After all, I may never see him again after tomorrow." Miriam had never seen her sister look so sorrowful.

"You don't have to leave, Harriet. You still have a week of your vacation. You can spend it here, and go home on the bus." She winked at her older sister. "Besides, I could use the help."

"She'll do no such thing!" declared Ruth Thompson. "Harriet is coming home with us, and that's the final word!"

"Why, Mama? What harm would it be if Harriet stayed a few extra days?" Miriam stared at her mother, color rising in her cheeks.

"Because, Miriam," the older woman said emphatically, "she has chores and responsibilities. Her place is at home with us."

"Ruth," spoke Ralph Thompson, "Harriet is a grown woman. She has every right to make her own decisions."

Harriet's fork dropped to her plate with a clatter. "I don't know what I'll do! I can't make up my mind!" The woman stood suddenly, her napkin falling to the floor.

"Sit down, Harriet, and finish your breakfast," commanded her mother.

"I'm not hungry, Mother." Harriet hurried from the room and stepped out on the porch, hoping the ocean breeze would help clear her head.

"Yoo-hoo," rang a musical voice from across the street.

"Good morning, Miss Nettie," answered Harriet, stepping across the street. Nettie Blackwell, dressed for 'early church,' was watering pots of red geraniums.

"Did you have a pleasant evening, dear?" she asked.

"Oh, yes, Miss Nettie. It was an evening I won't soon forget." Harriet sat in a nearby rocking chair, her face troubled.

"My goodness, dear, you don't *look* as if you had a good time." Miss Nettie was alarmed at the young woman's glum expression.

Harriet, rocking gently, stared at the porch ceiling. "I am surely in a dilemma."

Miss Nettie glanced at her watch. If she left now, she could slip into a back pew, and not be considered late. "A glass of iced orange juice and a bit of conversation may help."

Harriet smiled, "You are just what the doctor ordered."

Sitting at the kitchen table, a tall, frosted glass of juice before her, Harriet explained, "I'm faced with making a decision that could affect the rest of my life." Her finger idly traced the pattern in the oil cloth table covering. "I know I can't stay with Miriam indefinitely. If I don't go back to New York, I'll need a job and somewhere to live. I'll have to write a letter of resignation at the pharmacy where I work. Am I making a mistake giving up such a good position?"

"Hmmm," murmured Miss Nettie. "Why don't you go back to Miriam's, get ready for church, and pray that God will direct your path. That way, when you decide, you'll know it's the right direction for your life."

Harriet, relieved, patted the older woman's hand. "I'm going to do exactly that."

She rose to leave. Miss Nettie touched her arm. "You don't need to worry about a place to live. I have two empty bedrooms, and I'm tired of rattling around in this big house with only Barney to keep me company. Here you'd be close enough to help Miriam, and far enough to not hear babies crying."

After church, Harriet had lunch with John and his mother. Elizabeth Bell made Harriet feel at ease as she told anecdotes about John's childhood. The house, a cottage style, was located on Front Street, overlooking the water. "John's daddy told me when we were first married, he had to be able to look out his front door every morning, and try to see Portugal."

"And did he ever?" asked Harriet, smiling.

"No," answered Elizabeth, "but he seemed content just trying."

At three o'clock, the couple walked slowly toward town. "Your mother is so nice, John. Not once was she bossy."

John glanced at his companion. "I've been most fortunate, and I hope I've been a good son." They walked in silence, each dreading the farewell.

At Miriam's front door, John took her hand. "This weekend has been the happiest I can remember," he said, staring into Harriet's blue eyes. "Will you come again, perhaps next summer?"

"I'll try," she said, close to tears. *How awful a year without this kind man would be*, she realized.

When she stepped inside the house, her father called from the living room. "I want to talk to you, dear," he said. Harriet collapsed in an easy chair and stared at the ceiling. Never could she remember feeling so miserable.

"Harriet . . ." before he could continue, Ruth stepped in the room, carrying Emma.

"I'm certainly glad that man has gone home. You need to spend more . . ."

"Ruth," said Mr. Thompson, sternly, "You will have to be quiet if you want to remain in the room. I'm having a conversation with our daughter, and I don't wish to be interrupted."

Ruth Thompson started to speak, looked at her husband, and decided silence was best.

"Harriet, you look happier and more beautiful than I have ever seen you. I've never believed in love at first sight, but I think it is happening before our very eyes. John seems to be a fine, Christian man, and appears to be devoted to you."

The mother, unable to help herself, blurted, "Harriet can't stay. She has no job, and no money. Her small savings wouldn't last more than a few weeks. How could she pay rent, or buy food?"

Harriet looked at her father. "She's right, Dad. I haven't enough money to stay here."

"That's where you're wrong, Daughter. You have lived at home for several years, and paid rent to your mother and me. I have never spent a dime of it. There is a savings account in our bank in Binghamton in your name that amounts to several thousand dollars. There's enough to rent or buy a small house, and plenty to live on."

Harriet, dabbing her eyes with a handkerchief, hugged her father. "You'll never know how happy this has made me, Dad. I've made my decision, and I won't be returning with you and Mother."

"I hope you're satisfied, Ralph. Now our home will be empty. Harriet was our last," blurted the mother.

"That's right, my dear. Now I can take my wife on a second honeymoon." He winked broadly at his wife sitting across the room.

"Hello, Harriet. Do you have a minute?" When the young woman hurried across the street, Miss Nettie said, "Now, I'm not one to pry into other people's affairs, but I'm anxious to know if you are staying or packing." The older woman clasped her hands against her heart, never taking her eyes from Harriet.

"Miss Nettie, I'm wondering if your offer still holds. It looks like I'm going to be needing a room." Harriet stepped on the porch and embraced her friend.

"I prayed in church that God's will be done, but could He *please* let you stay."

Harriet threw back her head and laughed. "God answered your prayer. "Now I want to call John, and tell him."

"If I'm not being to nosey, what made you decide?"

Harriet thought a minute and slowly said, "The promise of a slice of Lillian Mathes' apple pie, with vanilla ice cream on top!"

Nettie Blackwell hurried inside her cool, spacious home and headed toward the telephone. *Jewel Mitchell*, she thought, *do I have an earful for you.*

# Chapter 10

"Don't cry, Amy," crooned her mother, holding the teary child. "Daddy has to go home, so he can go to back to work."

"I don't want him to go, Mama, cause' he won't be back for a long, long time."

"It won't seem long, Sweetheart," added her grandmother. "The time will pass quickly, because you'll be having so much fun."

"And," added the mother proudly, "Amy will be going to White Goose Nursery School in the fall."

"Oh, my," said Granny Jewel, eyes wide. "What a big girl you're getting to be."

Amy, momentarily distracted, "I'm going to school like my brother and sister. Mama is going to be home all alone."

Peggy rolled her eyes. "Yes, your poor mama is going to have to shop alone, read the latest best sellers, and work on projects I have put off for seventeen years."

Footsteps on the stairs caused all to look. James Bowers, carrying a brown leather suitcase, came slowly down the stairs. His sad expression matched that of the rest of the family. Amy wailed, "Don't go, Daddy! We want you to stay here with us!"

James reached for his younger daughter. "I don't want to go, honey, but Bowers Chemical can't get along without me."

Clara appeared with a brown paper sack, its sides bulging. She handed it to James. "This is just in case you need a snack on the way home," she said, winking.

James clutched the bag against his chest. "Thank you, Clara. I promise to take very good care of it."

When the car, carrying their father to Raleigh, was out of sight, Sarah turned to her sister. "Amy, how would you like to go swimming?"

Amy brightened. "Oh, boy! Oh, boy!" Her father's absence was no longer foremost in her mind.

Sarah turned to Joshua. "Would you like to come with us?"

"No, thanks. Mackie and I have to help unload a truck this afternoon. I don't have time for you girls."

"Suit yourself," said Sarah shrugging her shoulders. "We'll manage somehow without you."

Sarah was disappointed when they got to the shore. The tide was low, and instead of a shore line of white sand, there was a wide stretch of mud. Fearing another flood of tears, Sarah suggested they play along the water's edge. "We can build castles and draw pictures in the wet sand until the tide comes in."

The corners of Amy's mouth turned down, and her lower lip trembled. She looked up at her big sister. "Why can't we go in the water right now?"

"Low tide water is dirty," explained Sarah. "When the tide comes in, it brings clean water from the ocean. Sarah spread a towel on the dry sand and put a thermos of cold water and Amy's dry clothes on top. "Shall we make mud pies or a birthday cake?" asked the older sister, finding dead stalks of marsh grass for candles.

"Draw a picture in the wet sand," ordered Amy, tossing her blonde curls.

"I'll draw a picture, and you guess what it is." *You'll need a good imagination to guess my art work*, thought Sarah.

After guessing outlines of turtles, cats, dogs and rabbits, Amy sat down in a tidal pool. "No more pictures! I want to learn my A,B,Z's!"

"You mean A,B,C's," said Sarah, smiling.

Amy, digging her bare feet in the soft mud, answered, "Laney knows lots of her A,B,Z's. I don't want to go to school unless I know mine."

Sarah found a sturdy stick in the high tide line. "O.K., sister, school is now in session. The first letter of the alphabet is the first letter of your name." Sarah carefully drew an upper case A. Amy traced it with her finger. "Do more," she demanded.

"Let's do the second letter in your name. This is the letter, M, and the last letter in your name is Y."

Amy stood gazing at marks in the sand which represented her name. "A-M-Y, A-M-Y," she chanted. Sarah watched her sister as she began to understand the concept of symbols representing sounds.

"More, Sarah, more," begged the younger sister, "make more letters."

Sarah stepped to the right, and drew the letter 'S'. "This is a snaky 'S', Amy. It's the first letter in my name." Amy, on her knees, traced the letter with a tiny finger. Beside the S, Sarah formed the letter J. "This letter is J. It is the first letter in our grandmother's name, our brother's name, and our daddy's name." Sarah continued, fearful the mention of her father would cause more tears. She was relieved to see Amy too engrossed to miss her father. "The letter, 'J' reminds me of a fish hook."

As they moved along the shore, Sarah introduced more letters. "Now, let's go back and review what we have learned." Without warning, a strange feeling came over the seventeen year old girl. Standing barefoot in the soft mud, she stared, unseeing, across Taylor's Creek to the far shore. "This is what I want to do with my life," she murmured. "I want to teach. I want to see children's faces when they learn something new. I want to be the one to share that moment."

Amy yanked on her sister's hand. "They're all gone, Sarah," she wailed. My letters are all gone! The water ate em' up!"

Sarah scooped her sister up. ""They're not gone, baby sister," she laughed. "They're stored safely away inside your 'noggin.'. When we get home, I'll find paper, pencils, and crayons, and we'll play school."

"Can Laney come, too?"

"Sure! There's just one thing, I get to be the teacher!"

"You're gonna' have to find somewhere else to have your ding-dang school," announced Clara the following morning. "I can't feed this family three meals a day with paper, pencils, crayons and picture books on the eatin' table.

"It's not ding-dang school, it's ding-dong school. Sarah hurriedly stacked her school supplies and dropped them in a cardboard box. There was an envelope with pennies and Coca-Cola bottle caps for counting. Pictures from old magazines represented sounds and letters. "I'll set the table for lunch, Clara," she offered, hoping to appease the cook.

While all were enjoying a bowl of creamy clam chowder and cornbread muffins, Papa Tom glanced at Sarah. "Honey, you look tired. Have you been ironing all morning?"

Sarah smiled weakly. "No, Papa Tom. I've been teaching Amy and Laney their letters and numbers. I make up games to help them learn, and it's lots of fun, but it's a lot of work, too!"

Peggy smiled at her daughter. "I'm so proud you want to be a teacher, Honey. There's no more noble profession."

"Sarah will make a great teacher," added her brother. "Now she can get paid to be bossy."

"Sarah won't teach long," predicted her grandmother. "She'll fall in love and marry a handsome man and have children of her own."

Porter Mason's face flashed before her. *What's he doing this summer?* she wondered. *I guess he's working or taking college courses.*

"Sarah!" The girl blinked. "You were daydreaming," said her grandfather. "I called your name three times."

"She's dreaming about Prince Charming galloping up on a white horse and asking for her hand in marriage," teased Joshua. "He'll wish he only had her hand when he finds out how bossy she is."

"I'm going to keep *both* hands, little brother, so I can swat you!"

After lunch, Papa Tom tapped on Sarah's bedroom door. "Can you come down to the store, Sis? There's something I want to show you." Sarah, working on a lesson plan for the next day, closed her notebook and followed her grandfather.

They walked in companionable silence, enjoying the breeze from the ocean. When they reached the grocery store, Papa Tom paused. "What I want to show you isn't here. It's down *there*," he whispered. "Come on." They passed the Bank of Beaufort, Lipman's Department store and Pender's Grocery.

"We're about to run out of stores, Papa. I'm getting curious."

"It isn't much farther, my girl," Papa Tom assured her. He took her hand as they crossed Front Street and only slowed as they approached Paul Motor Company. "There's something inside you must see." Together, they peered through the plate glass window, their eyes resting on a cherry red automobile, decked out in a shiny silver grill reaching from headlight to headlight. "Sarah," breathed her grandfather, his hands cupped against the glass, "it even has a chrome bumper. Cars haven't had bumpers since before the war because there hasn't been enough metal. It's the first 'woody' I've seen in years."

Sarah cupped her hands against the glass to keep out the glare. She could see the sides were covered in fine grained wood. Wide, white sidewalls made the tires look like frosted donuts.

"I'm hopelessly in love, Sarah."

"Have you been inside to get a closer look?"

"No, I dare not. I'd lose my heart forever if I put my hand on that smooth metal."

Sarah glanced at her grandfather. "That's silly, Papa. How can a person love something made of metal, glass and rubber?"

"Hush, child, don't speak disrespectfully about such a heavenly machine."

"This is ridiculous! I've never seen you in awe of anything except Granny Jewel's temper." Sarah put her hands on her hips. "We're going inside and ask if we may sit in it." She grabbed her grandfather's sleeve and pushed open the wide double doors. For a moment they stood without moving in the spacious show room. On the walls were posters of the latest automobiles made by Chrysler Company. In the back were offices used by the salesmen.

"Look, honey. Have you ever seen anything like her?"

"Her?" whispered Sarah, gazing at the luxurious vehicle. "Why do you call it a her?"

"You just do, Sarah. I guess it's because a beautiful car can steal your heart, just like a beautiful woman." He took a step closer to the 1949 Chrysler hard top convertible. The red paint seemed to glow with life, the chrome mirrored their reflection. The interior was covered in smooth, creamy leather, the steering wheel in matching ivory with the Chrysler emblem in the center. Both stood, eyes closed, inhaling the distinctive odor of the leather upholstery.

"Might as well climb in, Tom," said a voice behind them.

"Phew, Halsey, you gave me a scare. I never heard you come up."

Halsey Paul, owner of Paul Motor Company, chuckled. "She has that effect on all men." He winked at Sarah. "Sit behind the wheel, Tom, and see what you think."

Slowly, the man put his hand on the silver door handle, knowing how a hooked fish feels being slowly drawn toward the boat. His hand dropped to his side.

"Go ahead, Tom, she won't bite," said Mr. Paul, eyes narrow, head cocked to one side. He took several puffs on a fat cigar and grinned. The smoke, creating a fog that seemed to fill the room, made Sarah cough.

"How about you, little lady? Slide under the wheel and see how it fits."

"No, thanks. If my grandpapa won't get in, neither will I."

"I'll have to think about it, Halsey. We'll come back."

Before Sarah turned to follow her grandfather, she glanced at the dash. It had a big radio with silver knobs, a glove compartment and other instruments she didn't have time to examine.

The pair hurried, as if they were trying to put as much distance between them and the siren call of the magnificent red machine. "Let's go to the store and barricade ourselves in the office," suggested Papa Tom.

"Hey, daddy, what were you two doing at Paul Motor Company?" asked Herb, as they stopped at the cooler for two Coca-Colas. "Are you getting ready to trade in the family fixture?"

"I don't have time to talk now, Herb," was the curt reply.

When they were safely behind the door of the office, Papa Tom blurted, "I declare! You can't do a thing in this town without everyone knowing it. If we wanted to take a little walk and window shop, it shouldn't be anybody's business."

Sarah sat across from her grandfather, straining to see him above the stacks of folders, letters and papers on the desk. He stared at her so long the girl became uncomfortable. She waited patiently, sipping her ice cold drink.

"Well, Sis, what did you think of her?" Sarah felt a rush of pleasure to know her grandfather wanted her opinion.

She thought for a minute. "Papa, I've never seen an automobile so beautiful in my whole life. I haven't seen one like it even in the city."

"The reliable cars are ones built before the war. But, the 1949 models are the best in several years. Our car is eleven years old, and I think it needs a rest."

"I think you deserve a new car," said Sarah with conviction.

"I agree, but what do you think your grandmother will say?"

"She may like the idea of a shiny, new car."

"Not just any shiny, new car."

"I know." Sarah sipped her drink. "It won't hurt to ask."

Herb Mitchell stuck his head in the door. "What are you two cooking up in here? Three different people came in the store wanting to know why you were seen going in Paul Motor Company. What am I supposed to tell them? Besides, I want to know myself." He stared without blinking at his father.

"Come in and shut the door."

Instantly, the young man stepped through the door, slamming it behind him. "What's up?" he asked, staring at his father.

"I wanted Sarah's opinion on a car Halsey has in his showroom."

Herb raked his hands through his curly, dark hair, a stray curl resting on his forehead. "Do you mean the cherry red, hardtop convertible with the wooden trim and leather interior?"

Papa Tom sat up straighter and glared at his son. "How do you know so much about that car?"

"Daddy, I walk past Paul Motor Company on the way to work, and when I go home for lunch. I have to stop and stare each time, and each time it gets prettier. Several of our customers mentioned seeing it coming into town on a car carrier." Herb's expression brightened. "Are you thinking of *buying* it?"

Tom Mitchell stood, pushing out his chest. "And what if I am?" he asked defensively.

"Mama would never let you have a car like that," answered Herb, laughing. He turned to his niece. "Sarah, you need to have a talk with your grandfather. He's got spring fever in July."

Sarah banged her soda bottle on the desk. "What do you think I need to tell him, Uncle Herb?" she asked, eyes narrow, lips in a thin line.

Herb was struck suddenly with how much his niece favored his mother. Before her steady gaze, he felt a vague sense of disquiet, much as he felt from his mother's penetrating eyes. "Well, uh, I can't imagine two old, or, I mean older people sporting around town in such a fine vehicle. Herb thrust his hands in his pockets, nervously jingling change. "It just seems a terrible waste of a fine automobile."

Papa Tom sat down heavily, and put his head in his hands. "You're right, Son, I'm too old to drive around in such a sporty car."

Sarah had never seen her beloved grandfather look so discouraged. He seemed to age before her eyes. Alarmed, she said, "Come on, Papa, let's go home."

In a soft voice, he replied, "You go on honey, I'll stay here and get caught up on some of this paperwork."

Sarah jumped up, walked around the desk and took her grandfather's arm. "Why don't we go talk to Granny Jewel. Red is one of her favorite colors."

The older man brightened. "I hadn't thought of that."

"Certainly not! The very idea, Tom Mitchell! Our dear old car is a part of this family. Why, the summer Sarah was six years old, you surprised us all by driving up in a shiny new car. The paint has faded, and there are a few rust spots, but that's no reason to abandon it."

"Jewel, the car isn't a part of the family. It's metal and glass, not skin and bones."

"Sarah used to sit in the back and sing little songs. It sounded so cute with her front teeth missing," said the grandmother, remembering.

"Come on, Jewel. "Let's take a ride downtown. There's something I want you to see," coaxed Papa Tom.

Sarah was still holding class when the couple returned a few minutes later. They remained on the porch instead of coming into the house. She could hear her grandfather's pleading voice, her grandmother's strident one. Moments later, the screen door slammed and her grandmother's footsteps were heard on the stairs.

"School is over for the day, girls. I need to talk to Papa Tom." Peggy emerged from the kitchen where she had been peeling potatoes for the noon meal. While the girls were clearing the table, Sarah asked, "Mama, how do you know when to get involved in someone else's argument?"

"That's an easy one, Sarah. The answer is *never*."

Sarah stared at her mother across the table. "Papa Tom doesn't act like himself. Is it possible a person can fall in love with an *automobile?*

"It happens all the time. It could also be a boat or an airplane."

"Has Papa told you about the car at Paul Motor Company?"

"No, but I have noticed he's acting mighty strange. He must be suffering from 'new car-itis.'"

Sarah grinned at her mother. "What is that?"

Peggy sat down at the table. "It happens to people all the time. You never know when it's going to strike. Years can go by, with never a thought of a new car, the suddenly, bang, you've got the disease. It can be triggered by your old car having too many problems, or just seeing a new car on the road. Once you get inside and smell the new car smell, you're hooked!"

"Poor Papa," groaned Sarah, "there's no hope."

Clara appeared in the kitchen door, drying her hands on her apron. "There's a cure for what's ailing your papa," she said with conviction.

"What is it, Clara?" asked the girl, eagerly. "We need to know before my papa gets any sicker."

Clara stepped over to the table and sat down. "The only cure for 'new car-itis,' is a *new car!*"

"Mama's not going to let him buy one," said Peggy, shaking her head slowly.

"He told me she wouldn't approve," said Sarah, feeling angry toward her grandmother. She brought her fist down on the table, set her mouth in a firm line, her eyes narrow. "There's only one thing to do, and that's to change Granny Jewel's mind."

Silence followed her remark. Clara's eyes grew wide. Peggy's mouth dropped open. "Nobody's ever been able to do that," stated Peggy.

"I think we should all three go upstairs and help her change her mind," declared Sarah, standing suddenly. No one moved.

"We have to help Papa Tom," pleaded the girl.

"You go first, Sarah, since it was your idea," suggested Peggy.

"No, Mama, I think you should go first, and do the talking since you're her daughter."

"Clara should go first because they have known each other longer than we," suggested Peggy.

Clara glared at the woman beside her. "You got any more bright ideas?"

Amy, busily coloring, closed her book and slid off the chair. "Where are you going, honey?" asked her mother.

"I'm going to tell Granny Jewel to let Papa Tom have a new car.

Sarah brightened. "That's it! We'll send the baby!"

"Where are you sending my grandchild!" came a strident voice from the hall. Startled, all began explaining.

"Stop! I can't understand if you're all talking at once."

Clara stood and hurried toward the kitchen. "I think I smell something burning.

Peggy turned, "What could it be, Clara? You haven't started cooking yet."

"I don't know," the cook added hastily, "but I'll think of something."

Jewel Mitchell strode into the room. "I smell a plot. Why don't you let me in on it."

"Mama, whatever gave you that idea?"

"Because, my dear daughter," she said, putting her arm around Peggy, "I am a veteran of countless devious plots and tricks." A resounding 'Amen!' came from the kitchen.

"Granny Jewel, sit down," commanded Sarah. When she obeyed so readily, Sarah almost forgot what she was going to say. "Uh, I love you and Papa Tom very much."

When she didn't continue, the grandmother spoke. "Your grandfather and I are well aware of that. Please continue."

Sarah began to feel uncomfortable under the steady gaze of her grandmother's blue eyes. "I don't like to see either of you unhappy, and right now, Papa Tom is very sad."

"It wouldn't have anything to do with an automobile, would it?"

"Yes, Ma'am. He has fallen in love with that beautiful car, but he knows you won't let him have it."

"That car is too gaudy. Can you imagine people our age driving around in the likes of that? It is a touring car, not a vehicle for going to church on rainy days or going out to Dolly Carraway's farm for milk and fresh vegetables."

She sat straight and gave a loud sniff. "Can you imagine what the people of Beaufort would say? We'd be the talk of the town."

"So what?" said Peggy, entering the conversation. "Half the people you know would think you're the 'cat's pajamas,' and the other half, well, they don't count. What matters most is, you and daddy being happy. Right now, Daddy is mighty unhappy."

Clara, her courage returning, added, "How about Emma and Eli? Are you willing for them to go to ride in an old, leaky, beat-up car that could die on the bridge to Morehead City?"

Jewel Mitchell turned and looked at Clara. "There are several new Dodge sedans on the parking lot. There is a dark blue one and a dark green one. One of those will do nicely."

Sarah shook her head slowly. "Uncle Herb was right after all."

Her eyes flashing, the grandmother turned her attention on Sarah. "What did my son say? I'm sure he sees his mother's side."

Sarah stood. "Uncle Herb said you were too old for a car like that." A deafening silence filled the room.

Jewel Mitchell leapt to her feet, the chair sliding backward across the floor.

"We'll see about that!" The others watched as she fled the room. "Tom," they heard her call, "what are you doing moping on the front porch? Let's walk down to Paul Motor Company. It's a beautiful day, and suddenly I'm in the mood for a ride in the country!"

# Chapter 11

"Sarah Bowers, you'll never guess who just rode past our house in a fancy new car!"

"Hello, Nancy. It's nice to hear your voice. Now, what were you saying?" asked Sarah, grinning.

"You heard me perfectly well. I was on the porch, and this gorgeous car cruises by and your *grandparents* wave and toot the horn! Well, you could have knocked me over with a feather! Mama's mouth dropped open so far, I was afraid she'd step on her bottom lip." Nancy paused for breath. "She insisted I call for details."

"My grandpapa bought a new car and they are trying it out."

"It seems such a bold automobile for people their age."

"I guess if you feel young, you might as well act young."

"Sarah, Mama is pointing at her watch, which means I have to say goodbye."

"Why don't we meet at Bell's Drug store for a dish of ice cream?" asked Sarah before her friend could hang up.

"I believe I still have a quarter in my purse. That will be enough for two bowls of ice cream—my treat. Oh, and Sarah," Nancy dropped her voice. "I know something that might interest you." There was a pause. "I know, Mama," Sarah heard her friend say. A moment later Nancy whispered, "Mama wants the telephone so she can spread the news about your grandparents' new car."

Sarah was curious. What information could Nancy have that would interest her? She had been coming to Beaufort for years but still didn't know many of the people. It gave her a sense of belonging to finally be plugged in to the information circuit of the small town.

Soon, they were sitting in a booth, stirring thick, creamy ice cream with a spoon. Both were taking dainty bites to make the ice cold refreshment last longer. "You have my full attention, friend," said Sarah, starring. "What is the big news flash you're going to share?"

"Do you remember Leland Davis? A few summers ago you saved him from getting in a lot of trouble."

Sarah glanced at her bowl, dismayed at how rapidly the ice cream was disappearing. "Of course I remember Leland. He saved Porter and me when we were attacked by a band of mean boys."

"Leland has been away at a special school studying photography. His pictures have won awards, his mother told Mama. He is supposed to be known for making people look natural in a portrait, instead of staring in a camera and grinning."

Sarah waited patiently, noting her friend's obvious pleasure in relaying this information.

"Well, Leland is back. He's opening his own studio on Turner Street."

"That sounds exciting. Let's walk over and see if he's there. Maybe he'll take our picture." The girls carefully scraped the last morsel of ice cream from their dish, and waved at John and Harriet as they filled prescriptions in the back of the store. They stepped out on the sidewalk, feeling the morning heat. "Phew," said Nancy, "it's hot enough to melt the South Pole. If Leland's there, we can get out of this heat."

When they turned the corner, Nancy asked, "Do you think there's a chance your grandparents will let you borrow their car? Think what fun it would be to cruise over to Atlantic Beach in a car like that."

Sarah laughed. "It may be awhile before I can pry my grandfather from under the steering wheel."

The girls peered in the window of the small, dark store front. "I don't think anyone is in there," whispered Sarah. "The place looks abandoned."

Nancy slowly turned the door handle. "It's not locked, Sarah. Let's go inside." The girls entered slowly, letting their eyes grow accustomed to the darkened room.

"Leland," Nancy called softly. "Leland, are you here?" They heard a noise in the back, and watched as a curtain separating the front of the store from the rear, parted.

"Is that you, Nancy?" the young man asked tentatively. "What do you want?" he asked, not unkindly.

Sarah noticed Nancy's tone change. She spoke slowly and evenly. "Why, Leland, we've come to see your studio. Will you show us around?" When he didn't answer, Nancy noticed he was staring at the girl behind her, so she stepped aside. "You remember Sarah Bowers. She is here during the summer but lives in Raleigh the rest of the year."

Sarah was surprised to see the once awkward, self-conscious boy had become a tall, nice looking young man. His sandy colored straight hair was combed back in a stylish fashion. "Hello, Leland," she said gently.

The young man stepped forward, and stood in front of Sarah. "You were my friend, my good friend."

"And you were a friend to me."

"If you two are through staring at each other, maybe you can show us the shop." Leland looked around, as if he were seeing the room for the first time. "I guess this is the office, and back there is the studio." He turned and led the way, holding back the heavy curtain.

Both stopped and stared. Inside the larger room were lights on tripods, a background scene of mountains, and a wicker sofa for clients. There were electric cords snaking across the hardwood floor and heavy drapes clinging to small, high windows.

"How's business?" asked Nancy doubt creeping into her voice.

Leland, looking at the floor, replied, "It's real bad, so far. The bank gave me a business loan to get started, but my daddy had to sign that he would make the payments if I couldn't. I sure would like to make enough money to pay my own way."

Nancy, chin in hand, tapped her foot. "Leland," she said as they returned to the front room, "this place looks more like Mr. Billy Adair's funeral parlor. In fact, Mr. Adair's office is a lot more cheerful. What you need are plants, vases, pictures, and a lot of other stuff. There's no name painted on the windows or an 'open' sign on the door. It sure wouldn't hurt to give the walls a coat of fresh paint." Nancy patted the young man on the arm. "In short, Leland, what this room needs is a 'woman's touch'".

Leland returned her look with one of confusion. "This room needs *what?*"

Nancy pretended impatience. "Oh, you know, silly! This room needs to be beautified. You can't expect customers to come in here when it looks like the inside of a cave." Leland looked around the room as if he were seeing it for the first time.

"Will you and Sarah 'beautify' it?"

"Oh, I think between Sarah's babysitting chores and my piano practice, we can find enough time to have this place looking like a Hollywood movie set."

"Do you think your parents will object?" asked Sarah.

"No, no," Leland hastened to assure them. "My mama thinks you're both wonderful. She'll like anything you all do. Our attic is full of stuff like you mentioned."

"I think the first thing we have to do is get some paint on these walls," offered Sarah, staring at a row of dusty, dark shelves.

"Go back to what you were doing, Leland, and Sarah and I will go down to the hardware store and get a couple gallons of paint and some brushes. We'll put it on your business account."

The young man appeared relieved, wearing a shy smile.

Back out on the sidewalk, Nancy asked, "Do you think he has changed? People used to think he was slow up here." Nancy touched her temple with one finger. "After you cleared his name in court, everybody started being nice to him. He wasn't so bashful after that, and when he went off to school, people showed him more respect."

"He still seems a little different."

"Someday, when he's rich and famous, people will say he's eccentric. While he's still poor and struggling, they will say he's 'different.'"

"Well, miss interior designer, what color are we going to paint the walls?" Both seemed relieved to talk of something else.

"How about white," suggested Nancy, thinking of the dreary appearance of the walls.

"White is too much like the inside of a hospital. Customers might start feeling bad if the room is too white."

"Light green?" suggested Nancy, trying to match Sarah's long stride.

"Nope. All libraries are painted light green. "It might get people in the mood to read a book, instead of have their picture taken."

"Blue?"

"No."

"Light Blue?"

"Double no."

"All right then, you choose a color. Think fast, because we're running out of colors," said Nancy irritably. They came to Beaufort Hardware and went inside. Mr. Clawson had a fan running in all four corners of the large room. Air was circulating, but the room was still hot and sticky.

"May I help you, ladies?" asked Mack Fuller.

"Yes sir, Mr. Fuller," said Sarah. "We need a color of paint for a new business in town. We want it to be dignified, colorful, inviting, and yummy."

"Hmmm," muttered Mackie's father, rubbing his chin. "That's quite a tall order. The girls followed as he walked slowly to the paint department. "My suggestion is a soft beige, or tan. It will be neutral enough for you to decorate in any style you like."

The girls looked at each other. "That's perfect!" breathed Nancy. Sarah nodded in agreement. "Oh, Mr. Fuller, do you paint signs to hang in the window to advertise what kind of store it is?"

"I'll be more than glad to paint a sign, or paint the name on the glass front." The girls decided on a soft beige, charged the paint to Leland, and started to leave.

"Stir that paint real good, girls. All the oil will be on the top when you open it."

Nancy held the gallon can in her arms, and Sarah carried brushes, stirring sticks and a bottle of turpentine for cleaning brushes. "He seems very nice," said Nancy and they hurried down Front Street. "Doesn't his son, Mackie work at your grandfather's grocery store?"

Sarah giggled. "Yeah, he works there. Papa says he's doing fine now. In the beginning, if he was sweeping the front walk, he'd curse at people if they didn't come in the store and buy something."

"That must have been awful for business," said Nancy, shifting the heavy can in her tired arms.

"I'm not sure. People may have been scared *not* to shop with us. Anyway, Uncle Herb convinced him that was not the way to behave."

When they opened the door to the studio, Nancy turned to Sarah. "Make a note—there must be a little bell mounted on the door to ring merrily whenever the door opens."

"You're back already?" questioned Leland as he stepped into the room.

"Yes, Leland. We enlisted the aid of a professional painter who suggested a soft beige, and we agreed." Nancy placed the heavy can on the counter. "Phew! That can got heavier with every step."

"You need a name for your studio, Leland," said Sarah. "Have you decided on one?"

"How about the Photo Shop?"

Both girls shook their heads. "Too vague," said Nancy.

"The Picture Store?"

"Never."

"Not in a hundred years."

"I give up," he said, and shuffled out of the room, head down.

"There now, you went and hurt his feelings," hissed Nancy. "You have to be very careful with Leland's feelings."

"You didn't like his suggestions, either!" Sarah hissed back.

Nancy thought a minute. "Come on, Sarah. I know a way to make this work." Sarah followed her friend into the back room.

"Leland, you know more history than the history books. Beaufort has been here a long time, even longer than Morehead City. Can you think of something from the town's past that would work?"

The young man dropped a cable he was working on. "Beaufort has pirates, British soldiers, and Yankees in her past."

Sarah noticed Leland spoke with confidence and seemed sure of himself when he spoke of the town's history. She remembered years before someone had said history was Leland's best subject in school. She felt if they could somehow tie the shop to the past, Leland would be more confident.

"Was Beaufort always known by its name? Was it ever called anything else?" Sarah asked.

Leland brightened. "Sure. It was called "Fish Town" before it was named for the Earl of Beaufort."

Sarah clapped her hands as Nancy squealed, "Fish Town Photography," they both yelled. "That's it!" said Nancy, skipping around the room.

She stopped abruptly. "We have already engaged a professional to paint the name on the window. Gold letters outlined in black would be sensational!"

Sarah frowned. "Why do you always have to sound so dramatic? Why can't you say we found a man that will paint the letters on the window?"

Nancy put her hands on her hips. "Because, friend, I am a very precise person."

"We'll see how precise you are with a broom and scrub brush. Every inch of this room has to be cleaned, or the paint will never stick."

"Do you have to help your aunt tomorrow?"

"That was the plan in the beginning, but as soon as Miriam's parents left, Granny Jewel took over. She or mama are over there almost every day. Mackie and Joshua are helping out at the store, so I am free."

Sarah walked through the house, her sandaled feet slapping against the hardwood floors. She paused at the kitchen door. "Clara," she asked, "where is everybody?"

Clara, adding strips of bacon to the top of a meatloaf, paused and looked up. "Well now, let me call the roll. Your mama and grandmamma and little sister are over at your uncle's house. Joshua and his grandfather are out joy riding in that fancy new wagon, and I was here enjoying a few minutes of blessed peace." Clara opened the oven door and slid the pan inside. Straightening, she turned to Sarah. "What's on your mind, my girl?"

Sarah related the morning's activities while Clara poured herself a cup of steaming black coffee. "I was wondering if I could borrow your scrub brush and a bucket tomorrow."

Clara's expression softened. "That's a mighty nice thing you're doing for that boy. Lord knows he could use a couple of friends." Clara opened a box of vanilla wafers and handed it to Sarah. "When that boy was born, his folks had such high hopes, but as the years went by you could tell he was slower than the other children his age. When he got older, the other boys teased and made fun of him. His parents hired special teachers to help him keep up in school, but . . ."

"Leland remembers everything written in the history books," interrupted Sarah, in his defense.

"After awhile," continued Clara, "people began ignoring him, and he kept mostly to himself."

"Mark my words, Clara," said Sarah forcefully, "someday people will come from *everywhere* just to have him photograph their children. Brides will insist on having him film their wedding."

Clara stirred her coffee, now cool enough to drink. "Having people believe in you is half the battle of getting along in this world. I'll be proud to loan you my scrub brush and bucket. And, I'm mighty proud of you and your prissy friend."

By noon, office walls, counters and display shelves were sparkling clean. The dank odor had been replaced with a clean, fragrant aroma. The girls scrubbed the floor last and warned the new renter of dire consequences if he set foot on it before it dried. All three stood in the entrance, admiring the transformation. "Mama told me to bring you home for lunch. She said for me to not take 'no' for an answer." He stared at Sarah. "I want you all to come, too."

"Your home is beautiful," said Sarah when they stood before a two story white house with double front porches. "You're so lucky, Leland. Every day you can look out your upstairs window and see Beaufort Inlet."

Leland stared out at sea as if he were seeing it for the first time. "You're right, but it's not a pretty sight during a hurricane. It gets a little scary to know there's only a few low islands between you and a real angry ocean."

The girls were faintly surprised to see the dining room table had been set for lunch. A white cloth covered the table, each place set with fine china and sterling silver. "Oh, Mrs. Davis, I'm afraid you've gone to *too* much trouble!" Nancy waved her hands in a dramatic gesture she had seen in a movie. "We would be more than content to sit at the kitchen table and feast on peanut butter and jelly sandwiches. I know it's not very ladylike to say, but, we are quite famished."

Ruth Davis beamed. "I'm glad to hear that, Nancy. Wilma and I have spent the greater part of the morning preparing dishes we hope you'll like."

Over a lunch of dainty sandwiches, fresh fruit, jello salad and iced tea, the conversation centered on the girls' families and their summer activities.

"And I hear your grandparents have a new car," Mrs. Davis said, smiling at Sarah.

"Yes, Ma'am." Sarah thought of how her grandfather bought a car yesterday, and today everyone in town knew about it.

"Have you driven it yet?"

"No, Ma'am. I'm afraid I'll have to wait until the newness wears off."

Wilma backed through the swinging doors separating the kitchen from the dining room. When she turned, all saw she was proudly carrying a three layer chocolate cake, with rich, dark brown icing glistening in the glow from the overhead light. She placed it on the buffet, and began clearing the table.

Nancy lightly touched the corners of her mouth with a white linen napkin, and turned to their hostess. "Mrs. Davis," she began, "we have agreed on 'Fishtowne Photography' as the name for Leland's shop. With Mr. Fuller's help, we chose a neutral color for the walls, and now we are seeking items for decorating the outer office. It needs to be businesslike *and* artistic. A coastal theme seems appropriate, since we live on the coast."

Nancy paused for breath as Wilma slid a generous slice of moist, chocolate cake before her.

"We would welcome any suggestions you may have, Mrs. Davis," said Sarah, hoping Nancy didn't sound too bossy.

"Fishtowne gives the business an historic flavor," said Mrs. Davis with enthusiasm. "Tan walls will make one think of the sand on the ocean's edge. Several oil paintings of boats and sea birds will help brighten the walls."

"Mama is an artist," added Leland, proudly. "A lot of her paintings hang in people's homes."

"Why don't we go up in the attic after we finish our dessert, and see if you can find anything you think would be suitable."

"This is a veritable treasure trove," exclaimed Nancy a few moments later as she stepped into the spacious attic room.

*Oh, brother,* thought Sarah. *It looks like a lot of stuff to me, but, to her it's a 'veritable treasure trove.'*

"Mrs. Davis," exclaimed Nancy, pulling a brass urn from the shadows, "this would be perfect with an arrangement of long-stemmed sea oat grass." The dim light bulb overhead showed a model of a sharpie sailboat.

"Who made this?" asked Sarah, dusting off the hull.

"Leland made that in high school. He carved the hull and I made the sails from white linen."

A large apothecary jar, filled with pink, tan and pearl colored sea shells was added to the collection.

Sarah moved in the opposite direction, drawn to several paintings propped against the far wall. She held them to light coming from a small window and found herself gazing at a nautical scene painted in oils. Sarah recognized Capt. Jake's boat house in the background, with rowboats tied to the dock. In the foreground were sea gulls resting on dock pilings. The next canvas caused Sarah's breath to catch in her throat. Through long winter months, Sarah kept a scene much like this in her heart and mind, knowing with the coming of spring, she would again stand and gaze across the channel to the distant outer islands.

A voice from behind startled her. "I can tell from your expression you like that painting. It's one of my favorite scenes," Mrs. Davis said quietly.

"Oh, yes, Ma'am! This is a perfect painting for the shop. Pelicans and shore birds diving for their dinner and banker ponies in the distance is the scene I keep with me all year."

Ruth Davis closed her hand over the one holding the painting. "It's yours, Sarah. I want you to have it."

"Oh, Mrs. Davis, I couldn't take such a valuable painting. It should stay in your family forever."

Ruth Davis looked at the young woman standing beside her. "I have never forgotten the day a little girl stood alone in court, and although threatened by bullies, testified in my son's behalf. If not for your courage, my son would have spent his life under the shadow of a crime he didn't commit."

Sarah held the dusty painting in her arms. "Thank you, Mrs. Davis. I'll hang it in my bedroom in Raleigh, and think of Beaufort every day." She smiled at the older woman. "I can't make a flowery speech like Nancy, but I am truly grateful."

"A flowery speech is that and nothing more. Actions say more than words."

"Hey, I'm finding perfectly gorgeous things while you two are talking!"

Ruth Davis winked at Sarah. "Sorry, Nancy, I guess we were falling down on the job."

The following week, all was ready for the opening of 'Fishtowne Photography'. The name was neatly painted on the window, and a silver bell, mounted on the door, tinkled merrily every time it was opened. One wall proudly displayed photos and ribbons from contests Leland had won. An oil painting by Ruth Davis hung above the desk. A large black telephone, typewriter and glass vase filled with sea shells sat on the desk.

Day after day the shop remained empty of customers. The last Monday in July, Sarah stopped in. Leland looked up eagerly when he heard the bell. "Oh, hello, Sarah. I thought at first you might be a customer."

Sarah put her hands on her hips. "Well, that's some way to greet a customer! I have come to make an appointment to have my portrait made."

Leland looked discouraged. "You're not doing this because you feel sorry for me, are you?"

"Of course not! Can't a girl get her picture taken if she wants to?"

Leland eagerly opened the new appointment book. "Hmmm," he said, scanning the unmarked pages. "How about tomorrow?"

"I think tomorrow will be fine. I don't have any previous engagements."

Leland slowly turned the crisp, new pages, stopping on one marked, 'Tuesday.' I have an opening at five o'clock," he said, looking up.

"Five o'clock? Is that morning, or afternoon?"

"Either."

"It will have to be afternoon. I can't see to powder my nose at five o'clock in the morning."

# Chapter 12

Sarah hurried along the sidewalk, her hair covered by a silk scarf. "Oh, brother," she muttered. "Why do boys have all the luck, and girls have to suffer?" Her question was directed at no one in particular, and perhaps no one would have a ready answer. The cool south breeze, so welcomed on other days, threatened to remove the scarf and ruffle the carefully crafted curls underneath.

Leland, seeing her coming, opened the door to 'Fishtowne Photography'. "You're right on time, Sarah," he said sounding relieved. He stood back and observed the girl as she removed the scarf.

"Phew, Leland," she said, closing the door behind her. "I thought the wind would blow me away. It has taken all afternoon to wash, dry, roll and comb out my hair," she said, starring in a mirror to check for damage. "I wasn't sure what to wear, so I chose one of my Sunday dresses." Again she peered at her reflection. "Is my lipstick on straight? I was afraid I'd be late, so I didn't apply it carefully."

"You look perfect," Leland said adoringly. "My car is parked in back. We have to hurry, or we may lose the sunlight."

"Hurry? Car? What are you talking about? I've come for you to make my portrait. Where are we going?" Not receiving an answer, Sarah followed as Leland disappeared through the back door, carrying his camera protectively in his arms. When she stepped into the courtyard behind the store, he was patiently holding the door open on an old pre-war Chevrolet.

"Where are we going? I don't understand."

"I'll explain everything on the way," he said hurriedly.

Sarah braced herself as they bounced along through town in the old automobile. At every stop sign the engine made wheezing sounds as they waited for traffic. Sarah noticed the headliner overhead was sagging and showed a network of stains where the car leaked. Glancing in the back seat, she saw a tripod and several satchels which she supposed held equipment for picture taking. Over the roar of the engine, Leland explained, "Portraits made in a studio are fine, but they don't look natural." He steered the old car across the bridge and out on the causeway. "I'm anxious to try out my new thirty-five millimeter camera with kodachrome film. It's the first time I've tried color film and I want to see if I like it." He glanced at his passenger as he turned off the causeway and headed the car toward the end of Radio Island.

"Is this where the new radio station is located?"

"Yes, and it's great being able to turn on the radio and hear music instead of static."

Sarah glanced at the young man beside her, and for a minute felt a vague sense of alarm. She didn't really know Leland that well, and besides, no one at home knew where she was. Sure, they knew she spent the afternoon getting ready to have her picture taken at the studio. Now, here she was, flying down a narrow strip of road in an old car with so many rattles, one couldn't talk without shouting. The man beside her was bent over the wheel, as if he were trying to coax more speed from the ancient vehicle. Sarah looked behind, hoping there would be at least one car following. Instead, there was a cloud of dust and sand billowing behind their vehicle. When it looked as if they would run out of road and topple in the inlet, Leland slowed the car, careful not to let the tires roll in soft sand. "I have to keep the tires on the hard surface. If we get stuck in the sand, the tires will sink out of sight, and we'll have a long walk home."

*If he's joking, I'm not laughing*, thought Sarah. There was nothing funny about the prospects of walking home in the dark. She got out of the car and looked around. They were on the end of a peninsula, surrounded on three sides by water. "My hair will be a mess, Leland," she said, dreading to get out in the wind. Sarah thought about the hours she spent with her hair in bobby pins, trying to coax a curl, or at least a bend in her straight, thick, dark hair.

Leland was already reaching in the back seat for his new camera. As he got out, he grabbed a straw hat with a wide brim. "We may need this for a prop." He looked down at Sarah's sandals. "Leave them in the car. You won't need them."

"Ok," she mumbled, "barefoot, stringy hair, wrinkled dress, and out at the end of nowhere. I can hardly wait to see the pictures." She hurried to catch up with the young man, who was already over the first low sand hill, moving toward the water's edge. When they reached the sandy beach, Leland pointed toward a rock jetty.

"Alright, Sarah, I want you to sit on the tallest boulder, and stare out to sea. Be careful not to cut your feet on oyster shells. We can't stop to bandage a cut and lose this late afternoon light."

*I guess it's alright if I lose a pint of blood, as long as we don't lose the light.* When Leland was satisfied with her posture and the tilt of her chin, he spoke softly. "Sarah, Portugal is three thousand miles east. Someone you love very much is there, and has promised to return. Every day you come here and search the horizon, watching for a ship."

Sarah tried thinking of each family member, but couldn't imagine anyone she knew returning from an ocean voyage. Unbidden, her thoughts turned to Porter Mason. She had neither seen nor heard from him in a year, yet she yearned to glimpse him standing on the bow of a boat, his dark red hair gleaming in the late afternoon sun. As the ship sailed into Beaufort Inlet, he would see her waiting faithfully.

"That's it, Sarah!" interrupted an enthusiastic voice. Her daydream shattered and was lost. "I snapped ten pictures, each better than the last."

Leland's enthusiasm was infectious. *I feel like a pin up girl on a calendar,* she thought. She waded out in the cool, green water, holding the straw hat in one hand and the hem of her skirt to keep it from getting wet in the other. The young man, pacing the water's edge, spoke encouragingly. "You're a little afraid of the water, but curious," he called, snapping pictures. Leland started telling silly jokes and Sarah began to giggle, then to laugh. She kicked a spray of sea water on a curious ghost crab on the beach, then spied an empty conch shell in the shallows. Picking it up, she held it to her ear and listened intently, her eyes once more focused on the vast ocean beyond the inlet.

"Sarah," called Leland, interrupting her thoughts, "it's time to go. We're losing our late afternoon light and I'm anxious to get back to the studio and develop these rolls of film."

As they were leaving, Leland spied an outcropping of sea oats growing along a low sand dune. Once more Leland's voice filled with confidence. "Sarah," he instructed, "go and sit among the sea oats. I think that setting has great possibilities."

On the way home, Sarah, cranked the window down and put her arm out to catch the breeze, her curls forgotten. She felt vaguely disloyal for being uneasy about coming to this desolate area with the gentle man beside her. "It's so beautiful over here, Leland. I wish I owned a house right on the edge of the ocean. Every day I'd sit on the porch, feed the gulls and watch the tide rise and fall."

"Yeah, and one day a hurricane would come along, and that peaceful water would rise up and float you and your house out to sea."

Sarah stared at his troubled profile, noting fear in his voice. "Leland, you look on the dark side of nature too much."

The car slowed, "I was six during the storm of nineteen thirty-three. People survived by climbing on the roof of their house."

Sarah noticed Leland was growing upset as he talked. "So," she interrupted, "when will the pictures be ready? I can hardy wait."

Leland turned the car onto the causeway road, and grinned at the lovely dark-haired girl beside him. The afternoon sun had brought a blush to her cheeks, her eyelashes long and dark. "I'm going to develop them as soon as we get back. All the chemicals and trays came in the mail yesterday and the darkroom is ready."

"Aren't you going home and eat supper first? I'm famished!"

"I'm not hungry. I'd rather develop this roll of film than eat a T-bone steak."

"When can I see them?"

"They'll be hanging on a clothespin tomorrow morning, dry and ready to frame."

Sarah tapped lightly on Nancy Russert's front door the next morning. She heard footsteps drawing near, and concluded Mrs. Cora was coming to the door. "Good morning, Sarah. What brings you out at such an early hour? Is everything all right at your house? Are your grandparents' well?"

Sarah stepped inside, unsure which question to answer first. "Uh, everything is fine, Mrs. Cora, I need to see Nancy, if she's awake."

Disappointed, the older woman pointed upstairs. "I haven't heard her stir, so you may have to wake her up."

Sarah quickly ascended the stairs and down the hall to Nancy's room. Sarah felt she was in a doll house when she visited. The windows of the upstairs bedrooms each had criss-cross priscilla curtains made from creamy white muslin. Wallpaper with delicate flowers on a cream-colored background covered the walls in every room. Dressers of dark mahogany had marble tops, and oval braided rugs were scattered across dark, polished wooden floors.

Nancy's dark curls contrasted with the snow-white linen sheets and pillow cases. The girl was breathing softly, unaware of anyone in her room. "Get up, sleepy head," teased Sarah. "There's something I want us to see."

Nancy groaned and turned her head to the wall. "I don't care if Clark Gable is sitting on my front porch," Nancy mumbled. She slowly opened her eyes and sat up. "If it is Clark Gable, I may reconsider." Now she came fully awake. "What do you mean, there's something you want *us* to see? Did you wake me in the middle of the night to show me something you haven't seen?"

"It's not the middle of the night, silly! Sunlight is streaming in your window, the birds are singing, and I'm anxious to see the pictures Leland took yesterday."

"Well, I suppose I can drag out of bed to see a picture of you all spiffed up in your Sunday dress and curls."

"That's just it, Nancy," she whispered. "The pictures were taken on the tip of Radio Island, with the wind trying to tear my hair out by the roots. I'm clutching a straw hat in one hand, and trying to keep my dress from flying over my head with the other."

"Move! I can't get up with you sitting on the side of my bed." She grabbed an outfit from the dresser drawer, and headed for the bathroom. "Keep Mama entertained with tidbits of news, while I get dressed." The girl disappeared in the bathroom and closed the door. "I'll be ready in two minutes," she yelled from the other side of the door.

Sarah hurried downstairs. Mrs. Cora was waiting. "Come out to the kitchen, Sarah and have some juice and toast."

Sarah followed obediently, knowing it would be futile to explain she had already eaten, and wasn't hungry. "Now tell me," started Mrs. Cora, putting bread in the toaster, "How is your aunt making out with those twins? I'll bet she's worn out. Does your grandfather like his new car?" she asked, pouring a glass of orange juice with pulp floating on top. "He must make up excuses to go on errands."

Sarah realized she had only to nod, while Mrs. Cora supplied questions and most of the answers. Before Sarah could finish a second slice of toast, Nancy appeared in the doorway. "Just toast for me, too, Mama," said Nancy sliding into a chair beside her friend."

"I should think not. You have to eat eggs, bacon, toast and juice to keep up your strength. How do you expect to play a concert grand if you don't eat?"

Nancy rolled her eyes. "Yes, Mama," she replied, unfolding a napkin and placing it in her lap.

Soon, the two were hurrying down Front Street on their way to Leland's studio. They heard the musical tinkling of a bell as they opened the door. The room, clean and freshly painted gave a much different appearance. Sarah's eyes were drawn to the wall displaying photographs that had won first place ribbons. Most were landscapes in Chapel Hill where Leland had attended photography school. The one which held

Sarah's attention was a fawn hiding in tall grass. It was staring into the camera with wide, brown eyes which seemed to plead for mercy as it remained where its mother had hidden it.

"Come on, movie star. I have to get back home and practice the rest of the morning." Nancy pulled Sarah by the sleeve and ducked through the curtain into the back room.

"Hi," greeted Leland, stepping from the dark room. His eyes rested on Sarah. "I have something I think you'll like," he said softly, opening the door to the dark room.

"Lead the way," said Nancy, stepping in front of Sarah. The only illumination in the dark windowless room was coming from a small red light bulb in the ceiling. "Hey, Leland, can we have some light in here? I can hardly tell whose pictures these are hanging on the clothes line."

Suddenly a burst of light flooded the room. "The light won't hurt them now, since they have been developed." All three stood silently before the pictures. It was obvious the young man had captured Sarah's quiet beauty. She stepped closer. The pose on the rock jetty showed a young woman wearing an expression of yearning and anticipation.

*Do I look like that whenever I think about Porter?* she wondered silently. *I must feel something for him I'm not even telling myself.* Hanging by clothespins beside that picture was a photo of her holding a white conch shell against her ear. She appeared to be listening, as one holding a telephone receiver. The late afternoon sun made her dress a deep and colorful shade of pink.

The last picture hanging above the trays of chemicals was the most arresting. Through a clump of long-stemmed sea oats, bowing gracefully from the sea breeze, a girl with enormous gray eyes, head slightly tilted, stared unsmiling, into the camera. Sarah stared back, unable to look away. "She has that effect on you, too?" whispered a voice from behind.

Sarah turned slowly. "Leland, I can't help it if that's me in the picture; I've never seen such beautiful colors in a photograph. Shackelford Banks looks close enough to touch, and the color of the ocean and the surf off Rough Point is perfect."

"If you're through admiring your work, Leland, I want to know when you're going to do *mine!*" For the first time ever, Sarah detected a note of jealousy in Nancy's voice.

Leland turned, "We can do it tomorrow morning, if it's not cloudy."

"Don't think for a minute I'm going out on that windswept stretch of forsaken land. *My* curls won't blow away," she answered smugly, glancing at Sarah, "but I don't want an uncivilized background for *my* portrait."

"I wouldn't dream of putting you in a picture with Bird Shoal as a background. I'll come to your house at seven o'clock tomorrow morning. Dress in simple, comfortable clothes like you wear when you're practicing your piano lesson."

"Won't you do it here, with a studio background?" questioned Nancy.

"Let me decide," Leland said sharply. "I want to capture the *real* Nancy, not just a girl smiling sweetly at the camera."

As they left the studio, Sarah turned to her friend. "I'm going to help Aunt Miriam today," she said, still smarting from Nancy's remarks. "Good luck tomorrow."

At seven o'clock the following morning, a light tap was heard on the front door of the Russert home. After waiting several minutes, the door opened slowly, and Mrs. Cora peeped out. She was pleasantly surprised to see Leland looking well-dressed and hair combed. "Good morning, Mrs. Cora. Is Nancy up?"

Cora Russell opened the door a little wider. "Come in, Leland," she invited uneasily. She was well acquainted with his reputation for being a little backward and never being able to 'fit in' with boys his age. Although hesitant, Mrs. Cora's good manners could not keep her from asking, "Would you like some breakfast, or a cup of coffee?"

"No, Ma'am, thank you. I ate breakfast with my mama before I left the house." He noted the look of relief on the woman's face when he refused. He had seen the look before.

The click of hard soled shoes on the stairs ended the conversation. Nancy appeared dressed in a starched dress with tiny yellow flowers. The collar and cuffs were made of sheer white organdy and lace. "Good morning, Leland," she said brightly.

Leland watched as she gracefully descended the last three steps. "That dress won't do," he said quietly.

Nancy appeared horrified. "What! This is my best and newest dress. Of course it's the one for my portrait!"

"No," insisted Leland. "The dress isn't right."

"Leland," said Nancy, "what's wrong with it?"

Leland sat back in the chair and studied his friend. "You're pretty enough without flowers and ruffles getting in the way."

Nancy couldn't think of an argument when someone had just given her a compliment. The mother remained silent, not sure how to respond.

"What do you suggest?" asked Nancy.

Leland studied Nancy's features, and then stared at the piano. Soft morning light filtered through delicate lace curtains, casting a glow on the fine furnishings and ornate decorations. His gaze returned to the girl. "Do you have a plain shirt, one that's soft like silk."

"Of course." Nancy spun on her heel and started upstairs.

"Hurry, Nancy, or we'll lose our light," called Leland. He looked over at Mrs. Cora. "I'm sorry, Mrs. Cora, but the picture is already in my head, and we have to get it right."

Mrs. Cora nodded slowly.

Soon, Nancy returned wearing a soft blouse of raw silk. A tiny edge of lace on the collar and pearl buttons were the only trim. Immediately, Leland was in charge. Gone was his bashful demeanor. With his prized thirty-five millimeter camera in his left hand he pointed where he wanted his subject to sit and how to pose.

Nancy sat on the piano bench, as if she were about to play. In a soft voice, Leland set the stage for the photo session. "There is a piano concert, Nancy, and tryouts are tomorrow. More than anything in the world you want to be a concert pianist, and winning this competition would be an important first step in your career." Leland's soft, smooth voice enveloped Nancy as he slowly moved about the room, searching for the right angle. Nancy's fingers rested on the ivory keys. She began slowly practicing her scales, growing more intense as Leland spoke of the very thing her hopes and dreams rested on. She became one with the music and her fine instrument. Fingers, nimble from years of practice, flew over the keys as the musician sought perfection.

Before Nancy finished her scales, Leland interrupted. "I have what I want, Nancy. I'm going back to the studio and develop the film."

By late afternoon, the photographs were ready. With gold picture frames from the attic of his home, Leland showcased several pictures of a young woman on a lonely beach. Others showed a young woman playing her piano, body rigid with concentration. A soft lace curtain, aglow with morning sunlight, bathed and illuminated her profile.

Another showed a lovely young woman whose expression told of her love and devotion for music.

The evening news over and the kitchen sparkling, the family escaped to the front porch, eager for a breath of cool air. Mary and Morgan Stewart, taking Laney for a walk, stopped by and sat down. "It must be exciting having a gorgeous model in the family," said Morgan, winking at Papa Tom.

Tom Mitchell gave his neighbor a curious look. "They're all gorgeous, Morgan." He waved his arm at all sitting in the rocking chairs. "Did you have a special one in mind?"

Morgan smiled at Sarah. "I'll have to agree, Tom, but only one is featured in the window of the new photography studio down town."

Sarah could feel heat rising in her face. "Papa, I told you Leland was going to take my picture. I'll bet you weren't listening." Sarah's words captured the attention of all.

"You say he has put her picture in the window of his shop?" asked Granny Jewel.

Mary's expression was serious. "Jewel, it's not just a picture. It's more than that. I, I don't really know how to explain it, but, it looks like Sarah could talk to you, and a prettier face I have *never* seen." She paused, "I'm thinking of having him do Laney's portrait.

"Well," sniffed Peggy, "If he's that good, I shall have him do Amy, too."

Papa Tom stood. "There's nothing to do but take an evening stroll past Fishtowne Photography and see what's cookin'."

"I'm going to stay here," announced Sarah. "I've already seen the pictures."

"I should say not!" exclaimed Peggy. "If these pictures are as lovely as people say, I want my daughter there so I can brag."

"People need to know your good looks come from your mother's side of the family," declared the grandfather.

"Oh, brother," Sarah mumbled, following her family. "It's going to be a long night."

# Chapter 13

"Peggy, dear," called Granny Jewel from the front hall. After a moment her daughter looked over the upstairs railing.

"Yes, Mama?"

"It's the operator, Peggy, with a person-to-person long distance call from Raleigh. I suppose it's from James."

Peggy hurried down the steps wearing a frown. "Why would James be calling me so early in the morning? I hope nothing's wrong." She hurried down the steps and took the receiver from her mother. Not waiting for the operator to speak, she said, "This is Peggy Bowers, operator." After a short pause, "James, honey, it's so good to hear your voice. Are you coming to Beaufort?" Peggy grew very quiet, a troubled look spread over her face. After several terribly long moments, she replied, "I'll start packing now and leave after breakfast."

Jewel Mitchell stood nearby, listening. Papa Tom slipped silently into the hall, waiting for his daughter to finish her conversation. After what seemed an eternity, Peggy hung up the telephone, and turned to her parents. "Granny Bowers fell and broke her hip. She's in the hospital and James needs me there. She'll need around the clock nursing care and it will be weeks before she can come home."

"Oh, my dear, that is dreadful news! How can we help?" Instinctivly, Peggy leaned against her father, his protective arm around her shoulder.

"Could Sarah and Joshua stay here? They still have a month before school starts, and I know they don't want to spend it in the hot city. I'll take Amy with me."

"You'll do no such thing, honey. Amy can stay here with her brother and sister."

Peggy looked doubtful. "Mama, you know Amy can be a handful."

"Amy will be just fine. Now hurry and get packed while I wake Sarah and Joshua. They'll need to tell their mama good-bye." Suddenly, the grandmother was in charge. "Tom, check her car for gas and water. Go and pack, Peggy. Amy and I will make a lunch for you to eat on the way." She took her granddaughter's hand and went to the kitchen. "Clara," she said, "Peggy has to leave for Raleigh as soon as possible. Mrs. Bowers fell and broke her hip." Granny Jewel continued through the kitchen and stopped at Sarah's door. Tapping lightly, she called Sarah's name.

"Come in," came a sleepy voice from the other side. When Sarah heard the news, she quickly put on an outfit lying across the arm of her chair and came out, tucking the shirt into the waist band of her shorts.

"Good morning, Clara," she managed as she followed her grandmother through the kitchen and into the dining room. "Have you heard the news?"

"Yes, Child, your granny told me. It's a sad thing to have to give up our children a month early. Old Clara's heart is breaking, but I know you have to go help your other granny." Clara voice, punctuated with sniffs, sounded more sorrowful than Sarah had ever heard. She stopped setting the table every few minutes and dabbed her eyes with a paper napkin.

"Oh, Clara, I guess I didn't make myself clear," Granny Jewel hurried to explain. "Peggy is going to Raleigh alone. The children are staying here."

Clara underwent an immediate transformation. "*Did I hear you right?*" she exclaimed. "Did you say the young'uns are staying *here?*" She clenched the napkin she so recently used to catch tears, and jammed it in the bottom of her apron pocket. "Raising three young'uns is a mighty lot of responsibility."

Granny Jewel gave a loud sniff. "Nonsense! These lambs won't give us a minute's trouble, will you darling?" she asked Amy, not sounding quite so confident.

"Come nightfall, you gonna' feel your age."

"It's only for a month, Clara. At the end of August, we can take them home in the new car." The grandmother smiled. "I know Thomas would love an excuse to sail down the open highway at fifty miles an hour."

Peggy appeared in the doorway, suitcase in hand. "Joshua is getting dressed. I'll grab a bite while I'm waiting for him, then I have to get on the road."

From the porch, Sarah stared as she watched her mother drive away. A feeling of loss and emptiness washed over her. *Why does it seem people say goodbye, more than hello? Saying farewell to someone you love is a worse feeling than being sick,* she concluded. She turned slowly and went back into the house. Her grandmother's lilting voice could be heard upstairs, its sound comforting. She took the steps two at a time.

"What shall we do today?" she asked, sticking her head in the door. Granny Jewel, making the bed with Amy's help, looked up and smiled. "I have an appointment to have my hair fixed, and I'm taking Amy with me." She watched as the four year old struggled with her side of the bed. "The child's hair has been in her eyes all summer. Those pesky barrettes work for about two minutes. With her mother gone, I'm going to see this child gets a *real* haircut."

"If Clara doesn't need me, I think I'll go over to Aunt Miriam's and help with Emma and Eli."

Granny Jewel rolled her eyes. "Oh, yes, I'm sure she will welcome you with open arms."

The screen door flew open as Sarah stepped on the porch. "Good morning, Sarah," said Miriam Mitchell. "You are a welcome sight!"

Sarah grinned as she stepped inside. "How are Emma and Eli today?"

"Truthfully, they are a bit fretful this morning. Neither Herb nor I got much sleep last night. It seemed one or the other was crying until morning. I was going to wrestle the baby carriage to the sidewalk and take them for a stroll."

The carriage, large enough for two, was parked in the wide front hall. It was kept in the Mitchell attic and brought down with each new generation.

"Aunt Miriam, why don't you let me take the babies for a walk? You can go back to bed for a nap, read, or call a friend. It will be a nice break."

Miriam looked relieved. "None of the above, my dear niece. What I want more than anything, is to soak in a tub full of bubbles for half an hour."

"Your wish is my command, Madam," said Sarah bowing.

"Sadie is dressing Emma and Eli in something cool since it's so hot outside." Minutes later, Sadie appeared at the top of the steps, a baby on each hip. Carefully, she descended, and placed a baby in each woman's waiting arms. When they were both safely tucked away in the fine old wicker carriage, Miriam hurried back into the house. She reappeared with what looked like luggage for a week's stay. "We mustn't forget wash cloths, clean diapers, water and milk bottles, tissues, and a change of clothes."

"Aunt Miriam, we're not moving away."

"You can't be too prepared, honey." The older woman stepped up on the porch. "Oh, Sarah, I almost forgot! John gave Harriet a huge diamond engagement ring. I'd like to give her a small tea to make sure she has met most of the ladies in Beaufort."

"Are they going to Binghamton to be married?"

"Oh, no! Our mother would take over like a commanding general and ruin everything." Sarah noted a hint of resentment in her aunt's usually soft voice. "They plan to marry in the parsonage of the First Baptist Church sometime in the fall, but have moved it up to the end of summer. It's to be a very small affair, with a big, long honeymoon!" Miriam smiled. "I'm so happy for my sister."

Sarah instinctively turned the bulky, white carriage toward Front Street and the ocean breeze. The rhythm of the tires bumping along the seams in the sidewalk soon had the babies fast asleep. "Well, that was easy," muttered the twins' cousin. "All I have to do is keep this carriage moving, until my aunt gets through soaking."

Sarah slowly made her way along the downtown area. Each person she passed wanted to peep at the sleeping babies and compliment her on her pictures in the window of Fishtowne Photography. Several admitted they had appointments to have their children's portraits made.

As they passed Mitchell's Grocery, the screen door flew open. "Who is this famous beauty, and what is her precious cargo?"

"Good morning, Uncle Herb," answered Sarah, grinning. "*Please* don't wake up your children. If you do, you're going to be in deep trouble."

Herb Mitchell's expression became grave. "They are only one month old, and in that short time, I have learned that silence is indeed golden, especially when babies are asleep."

Sarah jiggled the carriage, keeping it in motion. "Do you have a Coca-Cola on ice, Uncle Herb? My throat is parched." Two nights before, she heard a heroine on a radio drama use the very same words. As the uncle handed her an ice cold bottle of soda, Eli began to grow restless and fretful.

"Oh, I have to go, Uncle Herb. If they wake up, it's two against one, and the score will surely be in their favor." Sarah wrapped the bottle in a paper napkin and hurried outside. Carrying a cold drink while pushing the carriage proved to be awkward. "Phew, I need a time out, kids," she announced to the sleeping niece and nephew. She stopped the carriage under a tall oak, in front of the Inlet Inn Hotel and sat in the cool shade. "I'm going to sit under this tree and enjoy my soda, I hope," she informed the sleeping children.

After sipping the cool liquid, Sarah was startled by the sound of a voice nearby. "I know you." The deep resonant voice continued. "You're the beautiful girl whose picture is in the window."

Sarah's breath caught as she looked up into the bluest pair of eyes she had ever seen, their color accented by a deep tan. Curly blonde hair, bleached by the summer sun, bounced and quivered as the young man talked. In her whole life, the girl had never seen someone so perfectly fit the description of heroes in Greek and Roman myths. Surely Narcissus must have been this handsome. If so, it was no wonder he fell in love with his own reflection.

"Who are you?" asked Sarah, feeling the muscles in her throat tighten. She quickly sat up, trying to strike a glamorous pose, and stole another look at the tall, handsome young man. *Did he appear as if by magic?* She knew of no one in the town of Beaufort this gorgeous.

"My name is Lukas," he offered, gracing her with a radiant smile that dazzled girls half her age, and women twice her age.

"Where did you come from?" Sarah asked bluntly.

Lukas turned his head, showing a perfect profile. "I'm first mate on the Lovely Lady." He pointed to a gleaming white yacht anchored at the end of the government dock. "We're taking her to Martha's Vineyard to be outfitted with new diesel engines. We'll be coming back in December on our way to the Caribbean where we'll spend the winter." Once more he dazzled Sarah with his wide smile. "What's in the carriage?"

Suddenly Sarah wished fervently she wasn't babysitting. *Why couldn't she have met this handsome boy under different circumstances? If she met him at church, she'd have on make up and be wearing a pretty dress. Instead, she was still wearing the first thing she grabbed when she learned her mother was leaving.* "It's my niece and nephew. I'm babysitting for their mother. She had, uh, some things to do this morning." Reluctantly, the girl rose to leave. Lukas appeared disappointed.

He looked in the carriage at the sleeping twins. When he stood, Sarah was aware of how close they were standing. "Will I see you again?" he asked softly. He sounded as if his heart would break if they didn't.

"Maybe you could come by my grandparents' home this evening," she suggested, trying not to appear too eager.

"Do you live with your grandparents?" he asked.

"No. I live in Raleigh, but I'm staying in Beaufort during the summer."

"You say your parents are in Raleigh?" A wide grin spread across his face.

Suddenly, a wail pierced the air. "I have to go now, Lukas. It's time for the babies to have their bottle." She hurried down the sidewalk, vaguely embarrassed by the babies she so dearly loved.

"Hey, beautiful, I don't even know your name, or where you live."

Sarah looked over her shoulder and smiled. "My name is Sarah, Sarah Bowers, and I live at 509 Ann Street." On impulse she added, "Come by tonight if you don't have other plans."

If there had been wings on her sandals, she couldn't have returned any sooner. *I have to make it back before both set up a howl,* she decided. Miriam met them at the door, looking cool and rested. She eagerly took Eli and Sarah brought Emma inside. Each was given a dry cloth diaper while their bottles heated on the cookstove.

"Aunt Miriam," said Sarah enthusiastically, as she gave Emma her bottle, "I met someone while we were taking our walk." Sarah grinned and rolled her eyes. "He may come by tonight after supper," she said, suddenly shy.

"Tell me more, Sarah. This sounds exciting," said the aunt, giving Eli an extra firm hug.

"He doesn't live here. He's first mate on a beautiful white yacht anchored at the government dock. Aunt Miriam," she said enthusiastically, "he is the handsomest boy I have ever met. He just came right up and started talking." Sarah expertly swung baby Emma up to her shoulder and patted her back.

Miriam Mitchell's smile began to fade. "He's a crew member on a yacht?"

"Yes, Ma'am, he's the first mate," Sarah repeated proudly. Emma, now dry and fed, was placed in Sadie's capable hands. "I have to go. Lukas said he's coming by the house tonight, and I want to be ready."

"Six hours should be more than enough time," Miriam said wryly. "Sarah, promise me one thing."

"Sure," the girl replied, puzzled.

"Promise you'll introduce him to your grandparents before you go out with him. Your mother isn't here, and three grandchildren are a big responsibility."

A quick reply was on Sarah's lips, but she remained silent. On the way home, the girl seethed with anger over her aunt's last remark. *I suppose she thinks I'm a responsibility, like Joshua and Amy. It's funny I'm responsible enough to be trusted with her children. I can hold down a job at the grocery store, tend to my brother and sister, and help out at home. Now, I meet a really neat boy and everybody's jealous.*

Sarah hurried along the sidewalk, the madder she got, the faster she walked. "Well, well, look who's walking the streets of Beaufort on a hot afternoon.

Where do you think you're going in such a hurry?"

Sarah paused and looked across the street. A car was parked in front of Ma Baylor's house, the trunk open. A beautiful girl, making no effort to help unpack, started across the street. "Marnie!" exclaimed Sarah, happy to see her cousin for probably the first time ever.

"It's me," she announced, tossing her head of soft, blonde curls. "I'm going to be stuck in this town for the next two weeks." She cut her eyes at her cousin. "How do you keep from dying of boredom?"

It was on the tip of Sarah's tongue to explain how busy she had been helping with the twins and playing school with Amy and Laney. She knew from past experience her cousin would belittle anything she said. Suddenly, it seemed boring to her, too.

"I've been out with a lot of different boys this summer," said Sarah, unable to meet Marnie's steady gaze. *So,* she thought, *I have been to parties and socials at St. Paul's Church with other teenagers. There were a lot of different boys there. So I was sort-of out with them.*

"You'll have to introduce me," murmured Marnie, looking at her cousin with a new found respect.

"I'll be glad to, when I have time," said Sarah. It was such a change to have her cousin speak nicely, Sarah almost told of meeting someone new, but changed her mind. "I can't stop now, Marnie," she said airily. "I have a date tonight, and I want to wash my hair. It's so thick and long, it will take all afternoon to dry." At the corner she looked back. Marnie was still standing, arms folded, staring at her cousin.

"I couldn't get in the bathroom all afternoon," complained Joshua at dinner. "I finally had to go to the grocery store."

"Boys are supposed to pee in the yard," stated Mackie Fuller, incredulous Joshua didn't know this basic fact of life.

"Mackie, watch your language," warned Granny Jewel.

"Yes, Ma'am," he hurried to say, fearful he may lose his place at the table, and Clara's cooking. Each night, he carried a plate, filled with hot food, to his father. Since the death of Mackie's mother, two years before, Granny Jewel made sure they enjoyed at least one hot meal every day.

Papa Tom glanced at his older granddaughter, as he generously buttered a hot roll. "You look mighty fine, my dear," he said. "Are you going somewhere special this evening?"

Sarah smiled, "I met someone today when I was strolling the babies down Front Street," she said, suddenly shy.

Granny Jewel turned her attention from Mackie to the lovely girl sitting across from her. "Is this person a boy, or girl?"

"It's gotta be a boy, Granny Jewel," interrupted Joshua. "She wouldn't take a four hour bath for some old girl." Papa Tom nudged his grandson under the table, and slowly shook his head, a silent warning his grandson may regret wading into this conversation.

"It's a boy, Granny Jewel," said Sarah, glowing, "and he is more handsome than a movie star. And you know what . . . he likes me! We talked for just a moment, and then one of the babies began crying, so I had to leave." Resentment crept into her voice.

"Well! I hope we'll get to meet him. Who are his parents?"

"Oh, you don't know them. Lukas isn't from Beaufort. He's first mate on the big yacht tied up at the government dock." Sarah nervously stirred the food on her plate, appetite gone. She watched helplessly as her grandparents' expressions changed, resembling that of her aunt.

"We look forward to meeting him," said Papa Tom. "I want to see the young man my granddaughter thinks is more handsome than her grandfather."

After supper, Sarah combed her hair, put on a touch of rouge and lipstick, and brushed her long dark hair until it shone. When she was satisfied, she chose a book from several she had checked out at the library, and settled herself in a rocking chair on the front porch but found she couldn't sink into the new novel. If a car drove past, or someone walked by, she looked up, only to be disappointed. When shadows turned purple and became one with night, Sarah despaired of ever seeing Lukas again. Maybe his boat left suddenly, or perhaps he had forgotten the girl he met that morning. *He's so cute, I guess girls line up to meet him at every port.*

Stiff from trying to look casual for two hours, the girl decided to go inside. *At least I won't be supper for a million mosquitoes*, she thought. Giving a deep sigh, she stood and stretched.

"Sarah," whispered a deep, velvety voice from the shadows across the street.

Forgetting to act uninterested, Sarah threw her book in the seat of the rocking chair and hurried down the steps. Barely looking right or left, she stepped into the street.

"I'm over here, pretty girl," came the voice again. When she reached the other side, Lukas stepped out of the shadows. Light from the lamp on the corner made his curly blonde hair resemble a halo, his wide grin a contrast to the dark night.

"You're more beautiful than I remember," he said. "Walk down to the boat with me," he invited, standing close. I'd like to give you a tour of the 'Lovely Lady.'"

Sarah's heart hammered against her chest. *This is much too good to be true, she thought fleetingly. It has to be a dream.*

Lukas gently took her hand in his. "Come along," he whispered invitingly.

"OK, Lukas, but I'd like you to meet my grandparents. I told them . . ."

"I'm bashful, Sarah," he interrupted. "Meeting new people is hard for me." Once more he flashed his winning smile. "I'll meet them tomorrow."

The thought of seeing Lukas the next day thrilled Sarah. Fearing he would never return if she refused, Sarah let herself be lead along the sidewalk. Somewhere deep inside, she knew what she was doing was wrong, but felt powerless to stop. *Besides*, she told herself, *I'm old enough to make my own decisions. In less than a year I'll be the same age as my mother when she and daddy got married.*

Walking along beside the tall boy, Sarah tried to think of something to say so she'd have an excuse to turn and look squarely at the young Adonis by her side.

When they reached the dock where the sleek, gleaming white yacht was moored, Lukas slowed his step. "Having you here makes me happier than I have ever been." His arm expertly glided around her shoulders.

*This is more wonderful than a dream*, thought Sarah. *Being aboard the long, luxurious yacht on a cool summer night would be a delicious experience.* She imagined them sitting on the deck with a cold drink, staring at a new moon suspended in the summer sky.

Except for a small light in the forward cabin, the boat was shrouded in darkness. Sarah listened for voices of other crew members welcoming them aboard. The only sound was water gently lapping against the hull. She hesitated before stepping on the gangway. Once more the feeling of something being wrong crept into her consciousness, and once more she fought it back, determined nothing would ruin this perfect evening.

'Lukas," she asked, stepping on the upper deck, "where is the captain and the rest of the crew?"

"The captain likes to stay ashore when we're in port. The crew has gone to Atlantic Beach to enjoy the nightlife, and the owner is in New York. We only see him three or four times a year." Once more he slipped his hand in hers. "Let's go below and I'll show you the rest of the ship."

Suddenly, alarm bells went off in Sarah's mind. She was alone with a stranger in a place that was unfamiliar, and no one at home knew where she was. "I'd better not tonight, Lukas. It's getting late, and my grandparents will be worried." Afraid he'd be offended, she added, "I'd love to see the boat tomorrow."

Lukas looked doubtful. "We'll only be in port a few days," he said softly.

Sarah turned and started up the gangway, her feelings in turmoil. More than anything, she wanted to stay, but knew if she did, it would be wrong. She laughed nervously, "Besides, Lukas, my grandfather probably has the police department and the Coast Guard looking for me."

In the streetlight, Sarah saw him look anxious. "You're right. I better get you home."

Sarah had to almost run to keep in step when they reached the sidewalk. His smile and gentle way had vanished. She was glad to catch her breath when he paused near the house.

"Uh, why don't you go on, Sarah. I need to get back to the boat." He began to slowly step back.

"Lukas, I know my grandparents want to meet you."

Sarah remembered hearing the story of her parents announcing they were going to be married. Daddy stood with mama, but kept distance between Papa Tom and himself. He didn't abandon her to break the news by herself. Turning, Sarah was surprised to find that Lukas was no where to be seen. Filled with dread, she turned and walked slowly toward her grandparent's home.

# Chapter 14

The soft glow from a small lamp in the living room tried valiantly to penetrate the darkness. Sarah drew a sigh of relief. If everyone was in bed, no one would know how late she got home. Carefully she stepped her sandaled foot on the porch, avoiding a wide board that cried out when stepped on. Glancing in the window, she saw her grandmother reading by the dim light. Sarah had a sinking feeling she wasn't concentrating on the words in front of her. She slipped inside and hooked the screen door.

"You're up late, Granny Jewel," she said lightly, pausing in the doorway. Feigning a yawn, the girl eased toward the back of the house. "Good night." She turned and quickly headed toward the back of the house.

"Not so fast, Sarah!" Sarah recognized a seldom heard tone in her grandmother's voice reserved for someone in desperately deep trouble. It filled her not with dread, but anger. She turned and stepped into the living room. "Sit down, please," said Granny Jewel, her voice still firm.

Sarah slid into a chair, noticing lines on her grandmother's face were deeper, her expression weary. Maybe it's the lamp light, she thought. "Do you realize it's almost midnight?" Before Sarah could answer, "Where have you been young lady?"

One thing Sarah hated was being called, 'young lady.' The sound of it at seventeen years filled her with anger.

"In a few months I'll be eighteen years old. I can get married without my parents' consent, join the navy, or quit school and get a job. It's nobody's business where I was tonight, or who I was with." Sarah's voice rose, a contrast to her grandmother's now calm, authoritive voice.

"Young lady . . ."

"Don't call me that, now or *ever*! I hate it!"

"All right then, Sarah, as long as you are living under this roof, you must observe the rules we all live by. Being seventeen does not excuse you from practicing good manners."

"Nobody wants me to have fun! Today I met a boy that I like very much. Because he's not from Beaufort, and you don't know his parents *and* grandparents, you think he's not good enough to associate with us." Sarah felt a tear roll down her cheek.

"We waited up thinking we could meet him. When we started to bed, I checked the front porch, and you were gone. You disappeared with a total stranger."

"He's very shy," answered Sarah, lowering her voice.

"What's done is done," said Granny Jewel, feeling her sixty-eight years. "When he comes to call tomorrow, we'd like to meet him. Perhaps he'd like a home cooked meal. I'll ask Clara to prepare baked chicken, mashed potatoes, corn and butterbeans, hot rolls and chocolate cake. We want to make a good impression on this young man."

Sarah, wiping tears, mumbled, "I'm sorry, Granny Jewel for talking like that."

"I accept your apology, sweetheart." Rising slowly, she hugged her granddaughter and smiled. "I believe you inherited some of your grandmother's spunk."

Upstairs, Tom Mitchell lay in bed, eyes staring. Soon, he heard bare feet padding down the hall and into the room. "Papa Tom," said Joshua, pulling on his grandfather's pajama sleeve. "Something terrible is happening downstairs. You better get your gun and go see."

"It's OK, son, your sister and your grandmother are having a discussion. A gun is no protection against the pain of growing up. Go back to bed and pull the sheet up to your chin. Everything will look better in the morning."

The rising of the sun did nothing to dispel tension in the Mitchell home. Breakfast was a time when family discussed the day's activities and fellowshipped over ham and eggs. Today, all were silent. Joshua, remembering angry voices in the night, looked wide-eyed from sister to grandmother, fearful of what they might say. Papa Tom carried on a lively conversation with Amy about her new haircut.

"Are you sure your name is Amy Bowers? My dear wife took our Amy to the 'beautiful parlor' to have her hair cut, and brought you home instead."

"Papa, you know it's me." She held up a finger wrapped in a band-aid. "This is where I cut my finger on a shell. Don't you remember?"

"Oh, yes! You must be our Amy. Band-aids never lie."

The back door slammed and Mackie appeared in the doorway. "Good morning," he said cheerfully. "How is everyone today?" A cheerful greeting was required by Granny Jewel before he could sit at the table. He slid into his usual chair, immediately knowing something was wrong. *These people are never this quiet.* He folded his hands in his lap and bowed his head. "I did it, and I promise I'll never let it happen again. Will you all forgive me?" He looked up, waiting.

All eyes were on the newcomer. "What are you talking about, Mackie? No one has accused you of anything," said Papa Tom, puzzled.

With the side of his fork, the boy chopped industriously at his scrambled eggs. Staring at his plate, he said, "It ain't never this quiet in here, so, I figured you all were mad at me. I wanted to confess before my eggs got cold."

"No one is upset with you, Mackie," said Granny Jewel, soothingly.

"You ain't? Why not?"

"Why would you think we were?"

"Well, Ma'am, I do so much people don't like, I can't keep track of it."

A light tap on the front door interrupted Mackie's near-confession. "I'll see who it is," said Sarah, leaping from her chair and rushing to answer the door. Her voice, sweet and animated, drifted back to the dining room. The grandparents exchanged knowing glances. Moments later, Sarah returned, a look of pure joy written on her face. Behind her stood a tall young man with china blue eyes and a head full of soft, yellow curls.

*Mercy me*, thought Granny Jewel, *he is about the prettiest young man I have ever seen. No wonder my granddaughter has lost her heart, and her good sense.*

Sarah took the young man's hand. "Everybody," she said breathlessly, "this is Lukas!" She turned to the boy, "And Lukas, this is my family."

"We're pleased to meet you, Lukas," said Granny Jewel, smoothly. "I am Sarah's grandmother, and this is her grandfather." Papa Tom stood and shook Lukas's hand, pleased the lad had a firm grip. "Amy and Joshua are her younger siblings. Mackie is our guest."

Before she could invite Lukas to breakfast, Clara appeared. "Are you staying for breakfast, young man? I need to know so I can put your name in the pot."

"Clara," said Sarah, looking worshipfully at her guest, "This is Lukas."

"How do you do, now, sit yourself down. You look like you could use a square meal."

Lukas' hearty laughter was rewarded by a faint smile from Clara. In a short time, she appeared with a cup of steaming coffee. The guest stood as she placed it on the table. She was rewarded with a dazzling smile and a wink.

"Thank you, Clara. I haven't smelled coffee like this since I was in Jamaica," he whispered, as if they were the only two in the room. Tearing herself away from his gaze, she hurried to the kitchen to prepare a breakfast fit for a lumberjack.

"How long will you be in Beaufort, Lukas?" asked Papa Tom.

"We're waiting for a part for one of the engines. When that is replaced, we'll be going on to Martha's Vineyard. Both diesel turbines have to be overhauled, and then we'll be heading for the Caribbean. We should be back in North Carolina waters sometime around Christmas." He glanced at Sarah, giving her a lazy grin. "I hope I'll be able to see your beautiful granddaughter. That would be the best present I could ever hope for."

Alarm bells sounded in Granny Jewel's head. She looked at her smitten granddaughter, food untouched, staring at the young man as if no one else was in the room, or in the whole world. Well-oiled compliments rolled off his tongue as if rehearsed. How many other young girls on the eastern seaboard had been told the same thing? How many hearts had he already broken?

Clara appeared bearing a plate heaped with melon slices, eggs, bacon, grits and toast. She proudly placed it in front of Lukas, and stood back, waiting for his reaction. "Clara," he said, eyes shining," I will remember this moment for weeks to come, especially when we're on the high seas." He winked and smiled. "Maybe I can talk you into coming away with me and see the world."

"Don't waste your breath on old Clara. Both her feet are planted firmly on the ground."

*Yes,* thought Granny Jewel, *but little seventeen year old feet are not planted firmly, not yet."*

When breakfast was over, the family made no move to get up. "Granny Jewel, if you don't need me, I'd like to show Lukas around town." She smiled shyly at the boy beside her. "He promised to give me a tour of the 'Lovely Lady.'"

"If it's all right with your grandfather, Sarah. Please be home in time for lunch."

"Oh, Mrs. Mitchell, we'll have lunch aboard the boat, if you don't mind." Again, he dazzled Sarah with a broad grin and a slow wink.

Unable to think of an excuse, the grandparents consented.

After the boys left for the grocery store, Jewel and Tom Mitchell sat quietly, staring across the table. Clara quietly cleared the table and began washing breakfast dishes.

"Tom, should we call Peggy and James?"

"I thought of that, honey. What would we tell them, that their daughter is infatuated with a handsome stranger? It sounds innocent enough. She's the right age to be infatuated. Right now, they have their heart and hands full with Mother Bowers."

"They may decide to make a quick trip and take her back to Raleigh."

"Tom, can you imagine the firestorm that would cause? It would make last night's disagreement look like yoga meditation."

"Well, it's none of my business, but I'm going to put in my two cents anyway," said Clara, wiping her soapy hands on the hem of her apron.

"We'd like to hear your opinion," said Papa Tom.

Clara put one hand on her hip and rolled her eyes. "That's one fine looking fella, and used to turning girls' heads. Everywhere that boat ties up, I expect he trolls for young, unsuspecting girls. With that big grin and smooth talk, he wins their hearts. My question is, what happens when those engines start throbbing, and that white palace pulls away from the dock? I expect that pretty boy tosses broken hearts in the wind, and looks forward to the next port."

Tom Mitchell stood and slowly folded his napkin. "As usual, Clara, you have hit the nail on the head. Jewel," he said quietly, "the more we oppose this young man, the more appealing he will be. There is a solution, to this dilemma, and we must pray for it."

By the end of the week, Sarah was seeing Lukas every night. They went to the movies or walked the waterfront. At times Lukas would put his arms around the willing girl and steal a kiss. Days, he and crew members remained with the boat. On Friday evening they walked down Turner Street, stopping in front of Fishtowne Photography. Sarah's picture, staring through a growth of sea oats, still held a place of prominence. One of Nancy's pictures with the lace curtain in the background was also in the front. Now, several other photos had been added, all with different backgrounds and poses. Faces of children, concentrating on play, filled the window space. Sarah noticed Lukas staring in the well lit window on the other side of the front door. Moving over to see, Sarah was shocked by the ethereal beauty boldly staring back. "It's, it's my cousin, Lukas. It's my cousin, Marnie!" She glanced at the boy beside her, a trickle of fear forming around her heart. He seemed spellbound by the haughty beauty striking a sensual pose.

"Who did you say she is?" asked Lukas, sounding far away.

"It's my cousin from Greenville. She is visiting her grandmother for a few days." Hastily she added, "She's probably gone by now."

Still unable to look away, he said, "Why don't we go by your cousin's house and see if she's home. I'd like to meet her."

Sarah stepped back, fear, full blown, clutching her heart.

"Come on, my pretty Sarah," he cajoled. "I'm interested in meeting all members of your family."

"That won't be necessary," said a husky voice of pure velvet. Lukas turned slowly, catching his breath when his gaze rested on the owner of the voice.

"Hello, Marnie," said Sarah reluctantly. "This is Lukas Foster. He's first mate of the big yacht downtown."

Neither acknowledged Sarah. Their eyes were only for each other. Sarah noticed Marnie's hair was swept up in a sophisticated style, her makeup perfect. Pouty lips gleamed with shiny red lipstick, and long red fingernails flashed in the late evening sun.

"Naughty Sarah," she said in the same husky voice, her gaze never leaving Lukas, "why didn't you introduce me to your friend before now? Shame on you for trying to keep him all to yourself."

Lukas, finding his voice, gently chided Sarah. "You should have told me you had a beautiful cousin."

Sarah felt panic rise in her throat. "Lukas," she said, "We need to go, or we'll be late for supper."

For a moment, the boy looked confused. Finally turning to Sarah, "I need to go back to the boat for something. Why don't you go without me, and I'll be along later."

"I'll go with you, Lukas." She said helplessly. "It can't take too long."

"No! I mean, no, honey. I can go faster by myself."

Sarah turned to leave. "Bye-bye, Cousin," said Marnie, her voice merry. "Tell Aunt Jewel 'hello' for me." Her brittle laughter burned in Sarah's ears as she hurried toward home. Desperate to look back, she steeled herself against the impulse. In the Old Testament, Lot's wife looked back and became a pillar of salt. *Right now I feel like a pillar of stone, especially my heart.*

Granny Jewel and Clara were busy setting the table for the evening meal. When Sarah rushed inside, both could tell from her expression, the girl was upset. "Where is Lukas?" asked the grandmother, trying not to sound joyful by his absence.

"He forgot something, and had to go back to the boat. He may be a little late," she added.

Granny Jewel was alarmed by Sarah's expression. She had never seen her granddaughter look so distraught. "Is anything wrong, dear?" she asked innocently.

Sarah, ignoring the question, hurried to her room to change clothes and comb her hair. Clara turned to her employer. "I don't know much, but I think something strange is going on."

"Maybe God is answering our prayer."

"Or, maybe our baby is getting ready to elope."

The grandmother sank into a chair. "Oh, Clara, do you think she's packing? Do you think she's going to *run away?*"

Once more, the atmosphere at the Mitchell table was strained. Mackie, no longer fearful he had been caught doing something wrong, entertained the family with tales of how he had more marbles than any other boy in Beaufort school.

"I got this 'steelie,' and when it plows through a circle of marbles, they scatter! I come home every day with my pockets bulging. Sometimes" he offered, "if a marble I like don't get knocked out of the circle, I take it anyway, especially if the boy I'm playing with is smaller." Mackie's laughter died when he read troubled expressions on each face. "Of course," he added, worried, "I plan to give them back as soon as school starts."

"How do you feel after you have taken someone else's marbles, Mackie?" asked Papa Tom, not smiling.

"I used to feel good, but not anymore. Hanging around with Joshua, it's like my conscience is eating at me all the time. Stealing and cussing ain't as much fun as it used to be." He waited for a reaction from Mrs. Mitchell for using poor grammar, but none came. He watched the big sister as she glanced continually at an empty chair beside her, the place setting unused. Only Joshua acted normal, concentrating on a crispy fried chicken leg.

After supper Mackie went home while the family settled in the living room to hear the evening news. The day had cooled off and children's voices drifted in through the open windows. Sarah sat on the window seat where she had a full view of the street. During an ad about the nutritional value of Royal pudding, Sarah turned to her grandmother. "Something must have happened to Lukas. He's never been this late." She stared at her grandfather. "I should go down to the boat and check on him."

"Lukas is old enough to take care of himself, Sarah," her grandfather said sternly. "You have no business at the docks alone, and especially around that fancy yacht. They're leaving in the morning, and he's probably busy making preparations to get underway."

Slowly, eyes wide, Sarah stood and faced her grandfather.

"How do you know the boat is leaving tomorrow?"

"Because," interrupted Joshua, "me and Mackie grubbed her up today, and the captain told us this was their last day in port."

Jewel Mitchell's heart ached for her granddaughter. *Oh*, she thought, *if only I could bear her heartache.*

No longer able to listen to the comedy routine on the radio, the girl announced, "I'm going to bed."

Sarah, curled up in the middle of her bed, waited an eternity for darkness. When she was certain no one could see her, she slipped out the back door and down the driveway, avoiding the crunching sound of oyster shells under her feet. She ducked as she passed each window, and stopped at the corner of the house. The radio was still playing and each was listening intently. For a moment her resolve faded. *This is the last time I'll see my family if Lukas begs me to elope and marry him at sea.*

Suddenly, her mind was filled with thoughts of Lukas. Her beloved could be injured, and need her. When she was certain no one was looking and the sidewalk was deserted, she hurried across the street. At the corner, she avoided the circle of light from the street lamp. Turning, she made her way toward the waterfront. Before she reached Front Street, she spied Mary, Morgan and Laney Stewart coming her way. *They've probably been to the picture show*, thought Sarah. Darting behind a thick hedge, she waited impatiently for them to pass.

"What am I doing?" part of her wondered. *Two weeks ago if someone told me I'd be hiding in a stranger's bushes after dark, I would have told them they were crazy!* Part of her wanted to return to the safety of her grandparents' home, but, a force driving her from within was too strong. Characters in all famous love stories overcome any obstacle to be together. Propelled by this romantic thought, Sarah walked swiftly to the waterfront and onto the government dock. The 'Lovely Lady' sat peacefully at her moorings. The girl gave a sigh of relief. For a moment, she was frightened the boat might already be gone. Shrouded in darkness, Sarah could make out one dim light in the main cabin. She started toward the gangplank and was startled to see it wasn't there. In the faint light she saw it was on the boat, propped against the cabin. Fearing something terrible had happened, she called, "Lukas! Lukas! Can you hear me? Are you all right?"

Deck lights snapped on, blinding Sarah for a moment.

"Is that you, Sarah," asked the deep, smooth voice she had come to adore.

"Lukas! I was afraid something had happened to you when you didn't come to dinner."

Lukas stepped into the light, tucking his shirt inside a pair of white shorts. Effortlessly, he leaped from the gunwale of the boat to the dock. Instead of the warm embrace she had grown accustomed to, he crossed his arms over his chest. Slowly, he shook his head. "Sarah, sweet Sarah," he said, barely above a whisper, "You are a nice girl, and this week's been fun, but holding hands and looking at the moon is not *my* idea of how to spend a last night in port."

"But Lukas, I thought we were going to elope and have the captain marry us!" She grabbed his arm. "I love you Lukas, and want to be with you forever!"

Lukas glanced over his shoulder in the direction of the boat. "Look kid," he said, in a tone she'd never heard, "go home. There's no room in my life for 'nice' girls."

Sarah noticed he said the word 'nice' as if it were a terrible disease.

A voice drifted from the direction of the cabin. It was light and musical, one familiar to Sarah. A girl, holding a tall glass and wearing a towel appeared on the deck. "Lukas," she whined, "are you going to stand out there all night?"

"That's my cousin, Marnie," Sarah hissed. "What is she doing here?"

Lukas slowly backed away. "You have no business here. Go home, Sarah." He backed away, and turned toward the boat. Stepping on board, he disappeared below. The last thing Sarah heard was the merry laughter of her cousin.

Unable to move, Sarah leaned against the dock railing. This wasn't happening. It couldn't be. It was all a terrible mistake. Somehow, after a time, she realized Lukas wasn't coming back. She turned toward home, no longer trying to keep to the shadows. It didn't matter now if anyone saw her. Nothing mattered, or ever would again.

# Chapter 15

Sarah found herself standing in her grandparents' driveway, with no memory of walking home. The house was shrouded in darkness. All was silent. "They've gone to bed," she murmured. "I could have been in the middle of the ocean by now, and they'd still be peacefully sleeping." Sarah felt another stab of pain, her breath coming in shallow gasps as she remembered the brutal way her beloved had spoken to her. Walking down the driveway, she was surprised to smell cigarette smoke. *Maybe Ramie was here this evening,* she thought. Clara's nephew often stopped by to speak to his aunt, and blow smoke rings for Joshua.

Stepping quietly on the back porch, she was shocked and frightened to discover someone sitting in deep shadows. A glowing red dot explained the strong smell of smoke. "Who are you," she whispered, "and what are you doing here?"

"Sarah? Thank God you came back."

"*Papa Tom!*" she cried. "What are you doing out here in the middle of the night, and, and are you smoking a cigarette?"

"And, I might ask," said her grandfather, his voice strained, "what are you doing coming home at this hour?"

Sarah, stepping up on the porch, could no longer hold back tears that had threatened. She covered her face with both hands as deep sobs wracked her body. Strong arms suddenly enveloped her, producing a clean white handkerchief. Sarah buried her face in the soft cloth to catch her tears. The familiar smell of her grandfather's favorite shaving lotion gave her a small sense of comfort.

"Come over here and sit down." He guided her over to the bench where he had spent several terrible hours praying for his granddaughter's return.

"How did you know I wasn't in my room? How did you know I was gone?" asked the girl between sobs.

"When you told us you were going to bed, there was something in your voice that had never been there before. Somehow I knew. I just knew."

"Did you tell the rest of the family?" Sarah stared at her grandfather, waiting for his answer.

"What, and have your grandmother call out the Coast Guard and the Marine Corps? Half the town would have turned out to rescue the pretty clerk from Mitchell's Grocery. Why, Clara would lead the troops, brandishing her wooden stirring spoon and yelling threats." Sarah laughed, giving a loud hiccough. "I knew the 'Lucky Lady' wasn't leaving port until morning, and I prayed you'd return on your own."

Sarah leaned on her grandfather. "Luke doesn't love me anymore, Papa. He told me so tonight. He told me to go home."

"He doesn't deserve your tears, honey," said Papa Tom, putting his arm around her shoulder. Later, when tears lessened, Sarah made no effort to move. Starring into the darkness, she said, "Two days ago he told me he would soon be captain of the 'Lovely Lady,' and we would travel all over the world."

"What made him suddenly change his mind?" asked Papa Tom, thankful he had.

"He met Marnie this afternoon in front of Leland's shop, and changed completely. They couldn't keep their eyes off each other. When he didn't come to supper, I thought he had been in an accident. I was worried, so when everyone went to bed, I went down to check, and she was on the boat with him." Sarah continued staring into the darkness. "She took him away from me, Papa, and I'll hate her forever."

"Hate is a very strong word, Sarah. Someday Marnie's actions may catch up with her, and she'll learn her lesson the hard way."

Suddenly, Sarah turned and looked at her grandfather. She could see the outline of his face from the tiny light on the cook stove in the kitchen. "Papa," she whispered, "you were smoking a cigarette. Does Granny Jewel know?"

"No." A worried frown creased the grandfather's brow. "You're not going to tell, are you?"

"Your secret's safe with me. But, I didn't think you knew how to smoke."

The grandfather gave a deep sigh. "Only a few times in my life have I felt I needed to smoke. Tonight was one of them."

"Oh, Papa, I'm so sorry!" Sarah started crying again. "I thought you and Granny Jewel didn't want me to be happy."

"Honey," he said, patting her hand. "Your safety and happiness is foremost in our minds. There was just something about Lukas that didn't ring true. Your grandmother and I were very worried."

Sarah's shoulders drooped. "I'm tired. I think I'll go to bed." She rose slowly, patting her grandfather's hand. "I would have gone with him Papa. I would have followed him to the ends of the earth."

"I believe you, Sarah. I'm just thankful it didn't happen." They tiptoed inside, hooking the screen door. "Honey, don't sleep down here tonight. Grab your pajamas, come upstairs and sleep with Amy. Your little sister looks so tiny in that big bed since your mother left."

Sarah hugged her grandfather. "Thanks for waiting up, Papa. I needed someone tonight and I'm glad it was you."

"Honey, this is a rough time. You never love again as fiercely as you do at seventeen. Only time will heal the pain."

Sarah hurried to her room, grabbed a pair of pajamas and started toward the door. On her bedside table was her grandmother's Book of Common Prayer.

*There are a lot of beautiful prayers in here*, she thought. *Surely there are comforting words for someone whose heart is broken.*

In the bathroom, Sarah stared at the girl in the mirror. *How can I look the same on the outside, when I'm crushed on the inside?* She splashed cold water on her face, hoping the red around her eyes and nose would fade. The faint glow from the street light showed Amy in the middle of the double bed. Slipping between the cool sheets, Sarah curled her body around her sister's. Amy mumbled something in her sleep as Sarah inhaled the pleasant fragrance of bubble bath. *I'll never sleep tonight,* she thought, her head sinking in the soft pillow her mother used. The events of the evening crowded her mind. Turning on her back, she stared at the ceiling. Fresh tears fell, dampening the pillow.

Tom Mitchell eased onto the bed, hoping he would not awaken his wife. "Did Sarah come home?" she asked, no sound of sleep in her voice.

"She's home, honey, but she's in rough shape. That scoundrel dumped her for Marnie. Thank goodness the boat leaves tomorrow, and I hope he's on it—and he better hope he's on it. Maybe he'll take that tormenting girl with him. It would be good riddance to both of them."

"Tom, I never dreamed Marnie would be the answer to a prayer."

"Honey, with God, all things are possible."

A shaft of sunlight pierced the lace curtains and moved slowly toward the sleeping girl. When it reached her beautiful, oval face and tangled hair, its persistence caused her to awaken. Sarah eased one eye open. For a moment, she didn't remember the night before. "What am I doing in Mama's bed?" she muttered, her voice thick with sleep. Suddenly, the events of the night before engulfed her like the force from a powerful wave. The heartache and feeling of rejection flooded her conscious mind, reopening the deep painful wound. A pain in her chest, like nothing she had ever experienced, felt like a weight threatening to smother her. Turning from the sun's bright offering, she stared at the wall. The 'Lovely Lady' would be heading for open water soon, leaving Beaufort far behind. *I wonder if he regrets the things he said. Maybe he realizes he made a terrible mistake and knows I am the one he truly loves. He may be waiting on the dock, hoping to see me before he leaves.* Sarah sprang from the bed and dressed hurriedly. With scarcely a glance in the mirror, she flew down the stairs.

"Come and eat while the food's still hot," called Granny Jewel from the dining room.

"I'm not hungry. I'll eat when I come back," she called over her shoulder. Sarah flung open the screen door and bounded down the steps. It had never seemed so far to Front Street.

Almost out of breath, she prayed. "Please God, let the boat be there. Let me see Lukas once more." She turned the corner and stopped. Where the 'Lovely Lady' had been moored, there was nothing save a lone sea gull resting on a dock piling. Sarah stood, as motionless as a statue. *There's no reason to hurry now,* she thought, slowly walking out on the dock. She felt drawn to the place where she had last seen him, had heard his cruel words. Leaning on the weathered railing, she stared out to sea. Across the channel, banker ponies, their heads down, fed on an outcropping of tender grass. Shore birds swooped and dived on a school of minnows, and the sun, undaunted by the girl's sense of loss, continued its journey. Downtown, noises proved it was another normal work day. *Nothing has changed,* she realized; *nothing but me. I am different. My heart is broken, and it will never mend.* Sarah stared at the cool green water lapping against the dock pilings. *If I threw myself overboard and drowned, would he ever know? Would he be sorry he had caused my death?* Sarah leaned over the edge, comforted by the sight of the peaceful, blue-green water.

Someone grabbed her hand and yanked. Startled, she looked down. "Sarah, can we go get an ice cream cone?"

"Amy, what are you doing here? You're not allowed to *ever* walk out on a dock unless someone is holding your hand!" Sarah stared down in her sister's tiny face, all thoughts of the cool, green water erased.

"It's all right. Papa Tom let me. He says we can go to the Dixie Dairy in Morehead City and get an ice cream cone, if you will come, too." Sarah stared past her sister's pleading expression. Parked at the curb was the shiny new car, its white walled tires and gleaming red paint shining in the morning sun. Seeing her look up, he grinned and waved.

"Why is he driving his pride and joy? That car only comes out on Sunday afternoons."

"He said you might go if we went in the fancy car." Amy tugged on her sister's hand. "We don't ever get a chance to get dessert after breakfast, Sarah. If you won't go, I may never get another chance to eat ice cream, ever." She glanced up at her older sister, her eyes pleading. "It would break my heart in two."

Sarah shook her head. "Well, we can't have *two* broken hearts in the family, so, lead on." Amy happily pulled her sister by the hand and led her off the dock. In the car, Sarah turned to her little sister. "Amy, when we have Ding Dong School again, I have a new word for your vocabulary."

"What is it?" asked Amy, happy to be sailing over the bridge, every moment bringing her closer to the beloved ice cream parlor.

She glanced at her grandfather's profile. "The word is blackmail."

When Joshua came for lunch, he went straight to the kitchen. "Clara, do you know where Sarah is? I need to ask her a question."

"You can ask her one for me, too." Before the boy could ask what question, Clara continued. "I want to know what ails that girl. She acts like somebody sick with the flu; moping around the house, sniffing and sighing. She's been like this ever since that pretty stranger left."

The more she talked, the faster Clara's hands flew. Tuna fish salad was slapped on toasted bread at such speed, it was in danger of sailing across the room and landing in sticky gobs on the far wall. With age comes wisdom, and Joshua sensed the sooner he exited the kitchen, the safer he would be, to say nothing of the tuna fish salad. Tapping frantically on his sister's bedroom door, he was relieved to hear a muffled, "Come in."

"What's the matter, Sarah? Are you sick?" he asked, sliding onto the dainty chair covered in flowered fabric beside his sister's bed. He was relieved to see Clara had not followed. In this tiny room, there was no other exit, unless he felt compelled to dive through an open window.

He looked at his sister, curled in a knot in the middle of her small bed. *She must be seriously sick to look this bad,* he thought. "Are you sick?" he asked again, concern in his voice. "Will I catch it?"

Sarah laughed bitterly. "No, little brother, I'm not sick, unless you could say I'm love sick. I don't think there's much danger of you catching that."

"Did that boy from the boat do something to hurt you?" Joshua clenched his fist.

Sarah sat up and moved to the edge of the bed. Her clothes were wrinkled, her thick, glossy dark hair tumbling around her face. Red splotches around her eyes reminded the boy of a raccoon's mask. He started to comment, but wisely held his tongue.

"Joshua," the exhausted girl said, "when you are old enough to ask a girl for a date, please don't *ever* tell her anything but the truth about how you feel. Someday, a nice girl will fall in love with you. If you can't love her back, tell her so. Don't break her heart with lies."

Joshua, unable to imagine telling a girl *anything*, nodded solemnly.

"Are you young'uns through telling secrets?" asked a voice from the other side of the door. "Lunch is on the table, and I'm coming in."

"Come on, Clara," said the big sister. "I was just giving Joshua some advice on how to treat a girl when he's a little older."

"Well," said Clara, taking a deep breath. She pointed her stirring spoon directly at the girl on the bed. "It looks like you should have heeded somebody's advice. Your grandparents didn't approve of that boy from the start. Did you listen to them?" Without waiting for an answer, Clara continued. "No sir! Your mind was made up where that white trash was concerned. Someday a fine young man will come to call, either here or in Raleigh, and he will love you, and want to spend his life with you. I just hope you have enough sense to recognize the real thing when it comes along." Clara, her speech finished, turned and went back in the kitchen.

"Growing up gets harder every day," said Joshua quietly.

"You said it, brother. I used to envy you being a carefree little kid, but your life's going to get complicated, too."

"Amy doesn't have any worries yet, cause she's still little."

"Joshua, you came in to ask me something. Do you remember what it was, or did you forget after Clara's speech?"

"I wanted to tell you that this morning when you left, Papa Tom waited a little while, and when you didn't come back, he grabbed Amy right out of her chair and headed out the back door. Granny Jewel followed. 'Where are you dragging that child in such a big hurry?' she asked.

"I'm going to find our oldest granddaughter, and I'm using a younger one for bait,'" he yelled over his shoulder.' What I want to know is, what did he mean by that?"

"Wow," whistled Sarah. "I guess just because you're old doesn't mean life gets easier. Growing up is tough, but being a grandparent must be even tougher. Before they could continue, they were called to lunch.

"When is Nancy coming back?" asked Granny Jewel, adding pickles to her tuna sandwich.

"I think she was due to come back yesterday," answered Sarah. "Maybe I'll give her a call, and find out how she liked the mountains."

Relieved Sarah would have someone to help take her mind off Lukas, the grandmother nodded enthusiastically. "Cora will be busy on the telephone catching up on a whole week of news."

"After breakfast, if you don't need me, I think I'll go see Nancy. We'll be leaving next week, and I won't see her for the whole school year."

"Doesn't she come to Raleigh at least once a year to concerts?" asked Granny Jewel.

"Yes, Ma'am," said Sarah, smiling. "But, she's not much fun because all she can think about is the concert, and afterwards, all she can talk about is the concert."

"Nancy is a very serious student, and dedicated to her music. Is she planning to major in music when she goes to college?"

"Her dream is to go to Julliard, or Berklee in Boston."

"And how about my granddaughter," said Papa Tom. "What school does she plan to attend?"

For the first time a smile played around Sarah's lips. "Well, if I'm not going to be the bride of a handsome seaman, and sail the seven seas, I guess I'll apply to East Carolina College in Greenville. It's the best school if you want to be a teacher."

"Are you sure that's what you want, honey?" asked Papa Tom seriously.

"I can't imagine doing anything else."

Nancy greeted Sarah warmly. "I was getting ready to call you. I've got the ironing board up in the kitchen. Come and talk to me while I iron something to wear." Sarah followed her friend through the snug little house. "Has anything exciting happened while I've been gone?"

Sarah sat at the table and watched her friend. Every ruffle, seam and facing on each garment had to be ironed perfectly. Sarah thought of the times she had flown over her clothes with a hot iron, sometimes making more wrinkles than she removed. Sarah answered, "Uh, I met a handsome sailor who came to Beaufort on a big white yacht. He had curly blonde hair and the most beautiful sky blue eyes you've ever seen. It was love at first sight, and he asked me to run away with him and have the captain marry us at sea."

Nancy paused, holding the iron in mid air and stared at her friend. "Sure," she said, grinning, "now tell me what *really* happened while I was gone."

Sarah heard Mrs. Cora's footsteps on the stairs, and knew she was in for the third degree. "Why don't we go downtown to Bell's Drug Store and have an extra tall Coca-Cola?"

"What, and leave all this ironing while you tell more tall tales?"

Sarah stared at her friend. "I didn't tell you a tall tale. Every word of it was true."

Nancy gave her friend a long, careful look. "That sounds fine to me. Ironing is such a hot job." Nancy snatched the plug from the electrical outlet and placed the hot iron in the middle of the cook stove so it could cool, and with one swift motion, folded the ironing board, and shoved it in the pantry.

Cora Russert appeared in the doorway. "Good morning, Sarah. How are you today?" Without waiting for an answer, Mrs. Cora continued, "How is everybody at your house? What's happened since we've been away?" Sarah tried to answer the older woman's rapidfire questions while Nancy went upstairs to dress. In a matter of minutes she was downstairs waiting impatiently at the front door. "Come on, Sarah. Let's not take all day."

Outside, both girls breathed a sigh of relief. "My mama should work for a big corporation. She could be head of communications. Believe me, nothing would escape her notice."

"Or," added Sarah, grinning, "She could work for the army, and interrogate prisoners of war."

"In Raleigh, you know your closest neighbors and the people that go to your church. All the rest are strangers."

Nancy smiled at her friend. "Sarah, you don't know my mama. If we lived in the city, she would make it her bounden duty to know everybody and everything about everybody."

The girls shared a booth in Bells' Drug Store while they sipped their sodas. "Nancy, I wasn't making it up when I told you about Lukas Foster."

Nancy's eyes grew larger, her soda forgotten. "Tell me every detail. Leave nothing out."

Sarah drew aimless designs in the circle of condensation on the glass top table. "The day started like every other day. I went to Aunt Miriam's to help with the twins . . ." Sarah slowly and painfully relived the moments of the past week. The hurt, which threatened to smother her, returned, undimmed.

At first, Nancy clasped her hands over her heart and rolled her eyes. From time to time she'd murmur, 'how romantic,' or 'that's *so* romantic!' As Sarah related her last hours with Lukas, Nancy clutched the starched white front of her freshly ironed blouse, wrinkling the cotton fabric. So intent on Sarah's every word, the creases went unnoticed.

"I looked down into the cool green water and contemplated ending my life," whispered Sarah. "I thought if he ever heard I had thrown myself overboard and drowned, he'd be sorry for the hurtful things he said. I still feel I have no reason to go on living. My heart is like a rock in my chest." The girl sighed. "My family expects me to go on with my life as if nothing has happened. It's the hardest thing I've ever had to do." Sarah grew silent, resting her head on the back of the tall booth.

"I can't believe I was five hundred miles away visiting relatives when you were living your darkest hours."

Before Sarah could answer, Harriet Thompson stepped over to their booth. "Hi, girls," she said cheerfully, "It looks like your glasses are almost empty." Unnoticed, while they were talking, their glasses had become surrounded by pools of condensation. "Let me get you a refill," offered the older woman.

"How I envy her," whispered Sarah. "She is in love with a man who loves her back. Aunt Miriam says they're getting married soon, because they don't want to wait any longer."

"That's true," agreed Nancy, "but she had to wait thirty years to meet him."

"Phew! That's a long time," said Sarah, shaking her head. "You're almost old when you reach their age."

"Girls," said Harriet, returning with two tall ice cold drinks, "my little sister insists on giving me a tea before the wedding, and with the twins I think she'll need a lot of help. Would you like to be co-hostesses?"

"Oh, yes!" breathed Nancy. "I would do anything to help Mrs. Mitchell. She will always be my favorite teacher."

"Good. That's settled then. I'll call and tell her we have the situation well in hand."

After two glasses of Coca-Cola, the girls stepped out on the sidewalk. "Let's go by Leland's shop and see what he's doing. The poor guy is probably bored to tears. We can help him pass the time."

In front of the shop they paused. More pictures were on display in the front window, some unfamiliar. Sarah stared at the picture of herself holding a conch shell against her ear. She appeared delighted, as if someone was whispering a delicious secret. Sarah leaned on the glass, staring. *That's me, a lifetime ago. I had no worries and woke happy every morning.* Somehow, she could no longer relate to the carefree stranger on the beach.

The tiny bell tinkled merrily when they stepped inside the shop. For a moment their eyes had to become accustomed to the dark interior. Leland's voice could be heard in the back room, booming directions to a client. After waiting patiently for several minutes, they were rewarded with the shop owner sweeping back the heavy curtain.

"Hi, Leland," greeted Nancy. "Sarah and I stopped in to visit and help you pass the time."

Leland slowly shook his head, his eyes never leaving Sarah. "I'm sorry, but I can't talk today. I'm too busy. When I finish here, I have to do children's portraits. Could you come back another time?"

Slightly miffed, Nancy stood. "Leland, we'll call and make an appointment to visit before Sarah goes back to Raleigh." The girls found themselves once more on the hot sidewalk.

"Are our feelings hurt, Sarah?"

"No, silly. This is exactly what we wanted to happen. Leland has a life, and a career."

"Oh, look, in the other window there's a picture of . . ."

Sarah grabbed her friend's arm. "I can't look, Nancy. I already know who it is. Let's go back downtown and look in the store windows."

Nancy paused and shook her head. "I need to go home and practice my scales. I've been away from my piano a whole week."

# Chapter 16

Sarah watched as her friend hurried toward home. Alone, the familiar pain and emptiness returned. *I don't want to go home for awhile. I feel like a goldfish in a bowl, everybody pretending not to stare at the 'poor dear.' I'll go to the store and enjoy some of Uncle Herb's good-natured teasing.*

Stepping inside the grocery store, its sounds and smells familiar, made the girl feel better. The store was crowded with Saturday customers buying groceries for a week. In the back of the store she could hear the whirr of the meat grinder. Above the tall display case, she saw her uncle's curly dark hair. He was busily packaging meat while several people waited patiently. Mr. Case was at the checkout counter and had time for only a brief smile and wave. Joshua was bagging groceries and Mackie was helping people carry them to their car or truck. She walked slowly toward the back of the store, hoping she could find her grandfather. Through the glass door of the office, she saw him, head bent over an adding machine. *Maybe Mr. Case will let me check out groceries*, she thought, hopefully. *There's nothing like checking out a cart full of groceries to get your mind off your troubles.*

"Mr. Case," she asked, "could you use a little help?"

"Hi, Sarah. Thanks for asking, but we're doing fine. Enjoy your last few days of vacation."

"Yeah, Sarah," agreed her brother, busily loading groceries in brown paper bags. "Leave this job to us men folks." He didn't look up, so missed the deadly look his sister reserved for him.

Sarah stepped in the front door, letting it slam behind her. Knowing her grandfather would not be home before lunch, she curled up in his favorite chair and turned on the radio. Slowly turning the round wooden dial, she stopped the needle on a station playing popular songs. Leaning her head against the back of the chair, she closed her eyes. When the song finished, a voice announced, "Our next selection is, 'Slow Boat to China.'" Sarah listened as a popular crooner sang, "I'd like to get you on a slow boat to China, all to myself alone."

Sarah slammed her fist against the 'off' button. The silence was broken by her sister's high voice. "What you do that for, Sarah? That was a pretty song." Amy, eating an apple, looked curiously at her big sister.

"Because, Amy, the last thing I want to hear is a song about two people happily sailing half way around the world."

"I hope they don't sing a song about missing your mama, cause I miss mine."

"I miss my mama, too."

Amy stared at her big sister. "How come our mothers are the same lady?"

"We'll have a class on family trees in our next session of Ding Dong School. Now, go play. I don't feel like talking." Sarah turned her head and closed her eyes.

Soon, she heard a loud sniffle. When she opened her eyes, she stared into the teary eyes of her little sister. "I want my mama," said the little girl, tears spilling. Instantly, the sister scooped her up in her lap. Sarah felt tears stinging her eyes.

"Good gracious," said a voice. "Are there tears in my granddaughters' beautiful eyes? Why are my granddaughters unhappy?" Before either could answer, Granny Jewel continued. "I have a wonderful remedy for tears."

Amy, curious, turned to her grandmother. "What is it, Granny Jewel? How can you stop me from missing my mama?"

"It's a magic formula, and it works every time."

"I'm ready to listen," said Sarah, showing interest.

"When one is sad, or miserable, one only has to think of others."

"*Others!*" questioned both girls.

"That's right," said Granny Jewel nodding. "If you help someone else, you'll get your mind off your troubles."

"I don't know anyone who is as troubled as I," admitted Sarah.

"Sometimes you have to look. You'll never find someone who needs you if you sit in a chair and let your chin rest on the floor." Both girls grabbed their chins and smiled. "It just so happens," the woman continued, "there is someone who needs your help very badly."

"Who?"

"Who," echoed Amy.

"Nettie called this morning, and it seems she has pulled a muscle in her back and can't get out of bed. Dr. Maxwell stopped by the house on his way to the hospital and gave her some pills, but, she said they haven't helped much."

"How can we help?" asked Sarah, sitting up.

"Clara is fixing chicken and dumplings. We can take her a bowl. She may need errands run, and Barney needs exercise."

"I'll take care of Barney," offered Amy.

"I can run errands, and wash her car," said Sarah.

"That's the ticket! I told her we'd be along soon."

"We?" asked Sarah. "How did you know we would want to help?"

Granny Jewel stood and looked lovingly at her granddaughters. "Because, you are my blood and bone, also, your parents have done an excellent job rearing you."

"Yoo—hoo, Nettie," called Jewel Mitchell as they stepped inside her spacious home. A faint answer was heard coming from the back of the house. "Sarah, put the bowl on the kitchen table and we'll check on our friend."

The grandmother breezed into Nettie's bedroom, stopping suddenly. "Well," she said brightly, "you certainly don't look like someone who's ailing. You look like a glamorous movie star." Miss Nettie was sitting up in bed, layers of soft pillows in flowered pillow cases with lace edging banked behind her. Nettie's thick, curly hair was arranged in a single braid over one shoulder, a saucy bow on the end. The delicate odor of lilac cologne filled the air.

"Good morning," she said to each of her guests. "Please come in and sit down. Forgive me for not getting up, but my doctor said I needed bed rest, and dear Harriet insisted I follow his orders."

"I declare, Nettie, that girl has been a blessing. I know you'll miss her when she gets married."

"I will," said Nettie, sadly. "Barney and I will surely miss her."

"Don't despair. The Lord may put another needful person in your path." Granny Jewel looked around the room. "Where is Barney? Amy came to take him outside for some exercise."

Nettie looked out a window that faced the big back yard. Amy was sitting in the shade of a huge pecan tree, playing with the little dog. "Amy is already on task, Jewel. Now, tell me what's in that bowl I saw you take to the kitchen?"

"It's some of Clara's savory chicken with dumplings, so light and fluffy, it's a wonder they don't float out of the pot."

Nettie smiled at Sarah. "Tell me what you've been doing this summer, Sarah. I know your grandmother has kept you busy."

Sarah selected a chair near the bed. "I've been planning to come see you, Miss Nettie." Sarah smiled. "I've decided to be a teacher."

Nettie Blackwell reached for Sarah's hand and squeezed it firmly. "That's the best news I've heard in a long time. You'll never regret your decision. Oh, there will be times when you want to pull your hair out, but those times are quickly forgotten when you are presented with a bouquet of dandelions freshly gathered by precious hands. My favorite compliment was when my first graders told me I was the best teacher they ever had."

"Nettie, you need to rest now," said Granny Jewel, smoothing the already smooth covers, and once again adjusting the soft, fluffy pillows.

"Jewel," said the older woman. "you are a treasure, and my dearest friend, *however,* I'm going to have a nervous prostration if you make another adjustment to my already perfect bedding. I want nothing more than to talk with your lovely granddaughter. As teachers, we have a lot to discuss. Amy and Barney need to come in out of the heat, and I'm sure there's something you need to be doing at home."

"Well, I've never been told to leave before, but, I guess there's a first time for everything. I'll get Amy and we'll run along, if you're sure you don't need us," she said, sounding disappointed.

"Amy, I want you to sit at the coffee table and color a picture for me while I help Clara with lunch," instructed Granny Jewel, heading for the kitchen.

"I didn't expect to see you back so soon," said Clara, surprised.

"Any visit is going to be cut short if you're told you're not needed and to go home." The grandmother washed her hands and started slicing fresh red tomatoes and arranging them on a plate.

"You don't seem to be too upset."

"It's something only a best friend could do." When she finished the tomatoes, she began peeling fresh cucumbers. "It's really a blessing Nettie shooed us away, because on the way home," Granny Jewel paused, waiting for Clara to look in her direction, "I devised a plan to cheer up our girl."

Clara frowned. "I see that sparkle in your eye. It's the one that comes just before you start minding somebody else's business."

"It's not going to be like that this time. I have devised a plan I *know* will be successful."

"Maybe it will be like your plan to find your son a wife. That worked really well. Herb didn't need you shopping for him. He found a wife all by himself, and if I may say so, he did a good job." She paused and put down the knife she was using to slice ham. "I'm ready. Tell me your brainstorm before you bust a gasket."

"Well, Clara," she began, eyes sparkling," it has been ever so long since I've spoken to my dear friend in Canton, Ohio. I'm sure you remember Barbara Mason. Her husband was stationed at Cherry Point during the war, and they came back to Beaufort for a visit the following summer."

"Yes, I remember Barbara Mason. I'd say she was more like an acquaintance, unless that tall handsome red haired boy of hers is what makes her a *dear* friend."

"Are you insinuating I would call her just to inquire about Porter?"

"I'm not insinuating, I'm saying it right out loud."

"It could be that his name might come up, if I call her. After all, Sarah and Porter have been friends for years."

"It's getting along close to lunch time, so you better get on with your mischief." Clara arranged the ham slices on a plate. "I just want to go on record as being opposed to this operation. If it backfires, don't come crying to old Clara, cause I'm going to say, 'I told you so.'"

Jewel Mitchell marched to the telephone, keeping an eye on the front walk. Before she dialed zero for the operator, she spoke to Amy. "Honey," she said sweetly, "go in the kitchen and help Clara set the table. She really needs you."

The impersonal, monotone voice of the long distance operator came over the line. "Operator," Granny Jewel said firmly, "I wish to speak person-to-person to Barbara Mason in Canton, Ohio."

"One moment please," replied the voice. Soon, the grandmother heard the operator. "I have a person-to-person call for a Barbara Mason," said the impersonal voice.

"This is Barbara Mason."

"Go ahead, please"

"Barbara! This is Jewel Mitchell in Beaufort. How are you?"

"Why Jewel, what a surprise! It's wonderful to hear your voice. How is everyone in Beaufort?"

"Oh, fine. I realized today summer is almost over, and I hadn't heard from you all. I was hoping you were coming for vacation."

"It is so sweet of you to think of us. My husband is working long hours, so we haven't had a minute to think of getting away."

While Granny Jewel was listening, Clara eased into the hall. Seeing her, the grandmother looked away, unable to concentrate under such an accusing gaze.

"Uh, Barbara, you haven't mentioned Porter." At the sound of the boy's name, Clara rolled her eyes and mumbled something under her breath. "What is he doing this summer?"

While Granny Jewel listened, Clara whispered, "If you keep talking, the phone bill gonna put you in the poor house."

"Sarah is still here until the end of the week. I know she'd love to hear from him." There was another long pause. "That would be wonderful, Barbara. She'll be home all evening if he'd like to give her a call."

Granny jewel replaced the receiver. "Well, all we can do now is wait and hope."

"Hope you haven't opened a can of wiggly worms," said Clara, sniffing loudly.

At three o'clock, the screen door slammed. "Granny Jewel," called Sarah.

"I'm upstairs, honey."

A moment later, Sarah appeared in the doorway of her grandparents' bed room. "Miss Nettie and I had the most wonderful time," she began, sitting on the foot of the bed. Her grandmother sat at her vanity, surrounded by crystal bottles with fancy tops and tiny porcelain dishes which held such treasures as rings and fancy pins. There were fragrant lotions and creams her grandmother applied expertly. Powder, rouge and lipstick were applied last. Sarah watched, fascinated. As long as she could remember, it had been a treat to watch her grandmother perform this ritual.

"The chicken and dumplings were delicious. We each ate a large helping, and were scraping the bottom when Harriet came in with homemade cookies from John's mother." Sarah smiled at her grandmother's reflection. "Miss Nettie kept me in stitches telling one funny story after another of things her students said over the years."

Jewel Mitchell, relieved to see her granddaughter smile, sent a silent thank you to her best friend. Suddenly, Sarah's expression saddened. "After lunch, she told me her tragic love story. It was all I could do to keep from crying. That dear lady has spent her whole life remaining faithful to the memory of her fallen lover." Sarah sighed deeply, and shook her head. "I told her about Lukas, and how I, too, will never love another." Sarah stood, wrapping her arms around the tall bed post.

"There's one major difference, Sarah," said Granny Jewel wryly. "Owen fell in battle, defending his country. Lukas was a deserter."

"It doesn't matter what the circumstances are, Granny. True love cannot be denied."

*Nettie Blackwell, I'd like to give that long braid a good yank!* Granny Jewel thought. She spun around on the tiny bench, grasping her granddaughter's hands in hers. "You're right, honey. True love lasts a lifetime."

Sarah, tears threatening to spill, replied, "My hope is someday Lukas will return, carry me away in his ship, and we will spend the rest of our lives traveling the seven seas. I shall remain true to his memory forever, just like Miss Nettie."

Dinner was promptly at six o'clock. There was turkey with stuffing, mashed potatoes, hot rolls, and fresh string beans. Banana pudding topped with golden meringue waited in the kitchen.

"Boy, a white tablecloth, china and silver," noted Joshua. "Are we celebrating something?"

"Yes, Joshua. We are celebrating the gift of grandchildren. God has blessed us greatly."

"Amen to that," added Papa Tom. "Soon, your granny and I will have to look at each other across the table with a sad face." He bent down, chin almost in his plate, the corners of his mouth turned down.

Amy began to giggle, then laugh. "You're funny, Papa Tom," she shouted. Not to be outdone, the grandmother hid behind her napkin, wailing and crying, 'boo, hoo.'

"Hey, don't forget you still have me," reminded Mackie, attacking a mound of creamy mashed potatoes.

The laughter was interrupted by the ringing of the telephone. "Now who would be calling right at supper time?" said Papa Tom, irritated by having his act interrupted. He started to get up.

"No, no, dear! Let Sarah answer the telephone."

"I don't want her supper to get cold."

"It won't, Thomas. Trust me."

Moments before, the room was filled with boisterous laughter, now there was silence. "Yes, operator, this is Sarah Bowers. Hi, Porter! Yeah, it's me!"

Clara came in the dining room to clear the table. Never had there been such clattering of dishes and silver. "Clara, do you have to be so noisy?" asked Granny Jewel, irritated.

"Yes, Ma'am, I do. That telephone conversation was meant for one pair of ears, not a houseful."

*Seventeenth Summer*

As the family was finishing dessert, Sarah returned. All were amazed at the transformation. The glum, tragic expression had been replaced with sparkling eyes and a dazzling smile. "You'll never guess who that was!" she exclaimed.

Clara, returning to collect empty dessert plates, answered. "Well now, it wouldn't happen to . . ." She was interrupted by a sharp pinch on the leg.

"We can't imagine, darling," said her grandmother. "Tell us."

"It was Porter Mason, calling all the way from Ohio! He said he was sorry he couldn't get away this summer and come for a visit." Sarah, unaware, stirred her bowl of banana pudding until it resembled hand lotion. "You'll never guess what else he said." Before anyone could ask 'what,' she continued. "There is a boy on his hall at school that is from *Clayton, North Carolina*! Porter's going to catch a ride with him and spend Christmas in Raleigh!" She looked doubtful. "I hope it will be all right with my parents."

"It will be," stated Granny Jewel, firmly. "Trust me."

"He can be our house guest." Sarah took a deep breath and sighed. "Isn't that just the best news you ever heard?" Sarah leaped from the table and hurried into the kitchen. She returned with a calendar. "Let me see," she said, pouring over the pages. She looked up, alarmed. "Oh, No!"

"What's the matter, Sarah," asked Joshua.

"There are only one hundred days until Christmas vacation."

"That seems like a long time to me," said Joshua.

"You don't understand, little brother. I have a million things to do!"

"Like what," he asked mystified.

"My hair has to grow. Porter likes long hair. I must have a tube of red lipstick and matching nail polish. I need to lose five pounds, drink

211

a lot of water so my skin will glow, and buy a whole new wardrobe. Porter thinks I look pretty in pink, so I must have a new pink sweater." The faster she talked, the harder she stirred. The pudding in her bowl now was the consistency of tomato soup. Clara eased up behind her and cautiously removed it.

Eyes shining, the girl looked up at her beloved Clara. "Thank you, Clara. It was delicious."

"You are welcome, baby. I knew you'd like it."

"Special times call for special measures," announced the grandmother. "Tomorrow morning, you must go to Potter's Dress Shop and see their new fall clothes."

"Will you come with me? It's no fun to shop alone."

"It's no fun to shop with Amy. We couldn't concentrate."

"Don't worry about the baby, ladies. Amy can stay here and help me shell butterbeans. We may even have time for making a few mud pies in the back yard."

"I want to call Nancy and tell her the news."

"Sarah," asked her grandfather, seriously.

"Yes, Sir?"

"Suppose Lukas returns before Christmas to carry you away on the high seas."

Sarah looked thoughtful. "Hmmm, I don't think that's going to work. I'd probably be sea sick all the time."

In the kitchen, one scraped dishes, the other washed. "Sometimes you're right," said Clara, standing over a sink of fragrant soap bubbles. "Sometimes you're wrong, and once in awhile, you're a genius," she said, cutting her eye at her employer. "This is one of those times."

# Chapter 17

"I'm glad Mama called last night," said Sarah, the following morning, as she and her grandmother walked toward Front Street. "Amy seemed more content after she talked to Mama and Daddy."

"She'll see them Monday." said Granny Jewel sadly. She glanced at the low hanging boughs of a giant elm. "I don't know where the summer has gone. You all arrived in June, we turned around twice, and now you're getting ready to go back to Raleigh for your senior year."

Sarah caught her grandmother's hand. "Don't be sad. In a few years I'll come back and get a job teaching school at Beaufort High. I'll live with you and Papa, and be under your feet forever."

Granny Jewel smiled. "I'll try to wait patiently for that day."

"Good morning, ladies," greeted Virginia Potter at Potter's Dress Shop. "What can we help you with today?"

"Virginia, my granddaughter is returning to Raleigh on Monday. I want her to have a sweater, a very special sweater from her grandparents. It has to be pink." The grandmother glanced at Sarah and winked.

"You are in luck today. We just received a shipment of sweaters this week made of angora fur, and there is a pink one just Sarah's size."

Virginia led the women to a counter stacked with lovely cardigan and pullover sweaters of every color and weave.

"I don't see a pink one," whispered Sarah. "Most of these sweaters are dark, winter colors."

"The angora sweaters have to be wrapped in tissue, Sarah," said a deep voice, "because they shed so badly."

"Good morning, Mrs. Hendricks," said Granny Jewel. With barely a nod, the older woman swept past Granny Jewel and concentrated on Sarah.

"Now, dahlin' this navy blue with gray trim would be just lovely with your dark hair and gray eyes." Without waiting, she yanked the sweater from the pile and spread it on the counter. "I'm sure this would be very suitable for a school girl."

"No, Ma'am. I don't want a dark blue sweater. I want a pink one. It has to be pink."

"Now honey," continued Mrs. Hendricks, "Pink isn't considered a winter color. It would be out of season, and quite out of the question." Fearing a lost sale, the old woman pulled from the stack a dark brown cardigan with gold trim. "This sweater will never show dirt, honey. It will make a very practical wrap for school."

Sarah turned to the tall, resolute clerk. "Mrs. Hendricks, no other color will do. It *must* be pink." Virginia stood at some distance, admiring the girl who stood her ground against the formidable Mrs. Hendricks. She had seen women much older bow to the woman's bullying.

"Jewel Mitchell," she whispered, "you'll never die, as long as your granddaughter lives."

"I'm very proud of her in every way, Virginia."

"Very well," conceded the imperial clerk, "let's see what we have in angora." From under the counter, Mrs. Hendricks brought an armful of luscious, pastel colored sweaters, all wrapped in bands of tissue.

Never in her young life had Sarah Bowers felt anything so soft and wonderful as the sweaters knit from angora rabbit fur. Her hand sank slowly in the folds of a pale blue pullover. "This feels too good to be true," she murmured.

Mrs. Hendricks sniffed loudly. "These sweaters are not suitable for school, my dear. A garment made from angora would have to be reserved for the holiday season."

"Well, that's just perfect. I want a pink sweater for Christmas holidays. My boyfriend is coming all the way from Ohio, and I must have a special sweater, and only pink will do."

Mrs. Hendricks, unused to conceding, shook her head, turned and began searching for the required color. On the bottom of one stack, wrapped in soft white tissue, Sarah saw one a heavenly shade of pink. Slipping it out, she spread the weightless sweater on the counter. It had a dainty collar with tiny seed pearls sewn around the edge. Carefully, Sarah held it against her and turned to her grandmother.

"It is beautiful, honey," whispered Granny Jewel. "You must have it."

"Would you like to try it on?" asked Mrs. Hendricks, defeated.

"No, Ma'am. I know it's perfect."

"Do we have time to go by Aunt Miriam's?" questioned Sarah. "I'd love to show her my new sweater."

"We should have plenty of time. I don't have to help Clara for at least another hour."

"Oh, Sarah! That is the most beautiful sweater I have ever seen!" Miriam gently laid her hand on the soft wool. "It feels like the fur on a Persian cat." she groaned, "I won't be wearing angora for quite a few years. Can you imagine burping a baby with that on? Wrap it up,

Sarah, so I won't be envious, and come in the kitchen. We need to talk about the tea for Harriet on Saturday afternoon."

Sarah carefully wrapped her sweater in the tissue paper and returned it to the box, then joined the others at the kitchen table. "The twins are taking their morning nap, so we have a few minutes to talk, uninterrupted."

Miriam opened a tablet, filled with hastily written notes. "Sadie will be serving, and her niece will keep the twins upstairs."

"Why can't they be downstairs during the party?" asked Sarah.

Miriam looked thoughtful. "This party is in Harriet's honor. It's her day. If Emma and Eli are downstairs, all the attention will be on them."

"What are you planning to serve?" asked Granny Jewel. "Clara and I will be glad to bake something."

"Would you please make some of your famous pimento cheese sandwiches, cut in tiny bite sizes?"

"How many will you need?"

"Enough to feed at least forty women."

"Consider it done."

"Of course there will be peanuts and party mints, sausage balls and fresh fruit." Miriam looked at her mother-in-law. "Do you think that will be enough?"

"Yes, dear. Make sure there is plenty of ice cold punch. In hot weather people are more interested in a cold drink than something to eat."

While the women talked, Sarah stared out the window. *In five years,* she thought, *we may be sitting at this very table, planning a bridal tea or shower for me. Perhaps I will be engaged to a tall, handsome man who loves me very much.* Instantly, Porter's smiling face swam before her eyes, his red hair blown by the wind. *Well, tall, anyway. Amy, almost ten years old, will be my maid-of-honor. Emma and Eli can carry the rings on white, satin pillows. I'll buy a dress from the fanciest bridal salon in Raleigh. It will have lace dripping from every seam, and the skirt will have a million satin ruffles.* Sarah smiled at the vision of a dress that would resemble an overdone cupcake.

"A penny for your thoughts, Sarah," said Miriam, interrupting her daydream.

"Judging from her smile, they may be worth more than a penny," added the grandmother.

"I was just thinking that someday we may be planning *my* wedding. Granny Jewel, I want you to promise right now you will make my dress, and keep it simple."

"Simple and elegant, like Miriam's."

Miriam rocked back in her chair. "Oh, my! Sister's dress was a disaster, Mother Jewel, until your talented fingers turned it into a lovely gown any bride would be proud to wear on her wedding day."

Mackie tugged at Joshua's sleeve as the two hurried along in the late August heat. "Come on, Joshua. If we don't hurry, those women are going to have all the goodies eaten."

"No, no, Mackie. I know all about these things. Trust me. My granny and my mama take a notion ever so often and have parties. My daddy says it is a grand way to make new friends, and show off new clothes. He also says," continued the younger boy, "us men folks have to get as far away as possible, cause we're no match for a houseful of women all talking at once."

"I ain't scared of a bunch of women," grumbled Mackie.

"You wait. We're not there yet." When the two boys reached the Mitchell home, they hurried down the driveway and stepped up on the back porch. With their noses pressed against the screen door, they could see through the kitchen and into the dining room.

"Holy, moly," whispered Mackie, awestruck. "You're right, kid. I never heard so much talking at one time in my whole life." He started to back away and leave when his eyes wandered over to the long kitchen table, laden with trays of tasty morsels of food. "Wow!. This must be a dream. If it is, don't pinch me, 'cause I don't want to wake up."

"Didn't I tell you, Mackie?" asked Joshua, grinning.

"Why are you two hanging around Mrs. Mitchell's back door? Suppose she makes you come in and sip tea with the ladies?" Both spun around at the sound of the strange voice.

"Phew, Ramie! You scared me!" said Joshua, relieved. "What are *you* doing at the back door?" Joshua stepped over to his friend. "Did you come to get some goodies, too?"

Ramie slowly lowered himself on the top step and smiled his big, lazy grin. "I'm not interested in Mrs. Mitchell's goodies. I came to see that sweet confection that makes the goodies."

"What are you talking about, Ramie?" asked Mackie, puzzled.

"What he's saying, Mackie," said Joshua, feeling superior, "is that he's sweet on Sadie, Aunt Miriam's cook."

Ramie nodded slowly. "One of these days, I'm going to get enough courage to ask that pretty girl to marry me."

"Do you think she'd marry a one-legged man?"

"Mackie, that's not very polite!" blurted Joshua, afraid his friend's feelings may be hurt.

"You're a good one to talk! His wooden leg is on the mantle in your bedroom," blurted Mackie.

"That's OK, Joshua. I don't mind answering Mackie's question. The truth is, I don't know, but I aim to find out." Ramie reached in his shirt pocket and brought out a pack of Lucky Strike cigarettes. Both boys watched in fascination as the older man blew perfect smoke rings around them. Forgotten were the ladies and the goodies.

"Show me how to do that, Ramie," said Mackie.

"Someday, when you're older, I'll show you."

"Older? I know how to smoke now. I just don't smoke around my little conscience here, or he'll give me a lecture."

Suddenly the screen door flew open. "Ramie," said Miriam Mitchell, "Thank goodness you're here! The lid was left off the ice box in the pantry, and all the ice has melted! I can't let the guests drink warm lemonade. Would you go to the ice house and get a huge chunk of ice?"

"Don't worry, Mrs. Mitchell. You'll have ice right away."

Looking relieved, Miriam disappeared in the house. A moment later, she brought a dollar bill out, and pressed it into Ramie's hand. "Thank you," she whispered.

Ramie looked down at the two boys sitting on the steps. "Boys," he began, "this artificial leg slows me down, and your aunt needs ice *now.*" He looked solemn. "You could do the job in half the time."

"All right!" shouted the boys. Joshua took the dollar and they hurried around the house. Before they reached the street, he felt someone tugging at his shirt.

"Whoa, Nellie," said Mackie. "A dollar's worth of ice is going to be the size of an iceberg. By the time we take turns toting it through the streets, it'll be so small, it won't cool a glass of iced tea." A sly smile came over the older boy's face. Joshua had seen that expression before, and knew it could mean trouble.

"What are you thinking?" he asked cautiously.

Mackie pointed at the lovely old wicker baby carriage sitting sedately on the front porch, ready to take Emma and Eli on an afternoon outing.

"That's for babies, not ice."

"Nobody will ever know. Your aunt, sister, and grandmother are too busy to notice. People passing will think we're taking the babies out for a stroll."

Joshua shook his head, trying to imagine Aunt Miriam entrusting her children to the tough talking, hard hitting lad. Before he could think of an excuse, his friend was on the porch, banging the carriage down the steps.

"We gonna be heroes when we get back with a block of ice big enough to freeze a battle ship." Joshua hurried to keep up with his friend as he jogged along the uneven sidewalk. With every rut and pothole, the fine old carriage creaked and groaned in protest. Spokes in the wheels were the first to come apart, sticking out at a strange angle. When they reached the ice house at the end of Craven Street, Mackie parked the carriage at the edge of a tall ramp. A man stepped out of the dark doorway, vapor forming from the cold air inside.

"Well, lookie here," he said, grinning. "If it isn't two little ladies out strolling their baby. Which one is the mother?" Laughing at his own joke, Joshua saw several teeth missing. He was wearing a coat, which seemed strange on a hot summer day, his head wet from condensation.

"That's not funny, mister. We need a dollar's worth of ice, and we need it *fast!*" The man turned and went inside the cavernous building, scuffing his heels along the floor covered in sawdust. Soon, he came out, pushing a huge block of ice on a small cart whose wheels squealed from the weight. With a pair of huge, rusty ice tongs he shifted the block from the cart to the graceful carriage. The weight from the ice caused it to sag dangerously. "Here, Mister," said Mackie. He handed the man the wadded dollar bill and turned the carriage around. "Come on, Joshua. We gotta make hay while the sun shines, or, we gotta make hay while the ice melts."

Both had to push the carriage with such a heavy load. At each curb, Mackie lifted the front while Joshua pushed with all his strength, alarmed to see pieces of white wicker popping off the sides. As they wrestled the carriage up on the last curbing, Mackie, tired, gave a mighty yank on the top. It came away in his hands, almost causing him to fall. "We're gonna get this thing to your aunt's house if it's the last thing we ever do."

"It's the last thing this carriage is gonna do," observed Joshua. "The wheels wobble so bad, I can't hardly steer it. It'll be a miracle if we make it that far." With one pulling, and one pushing, they finally arrived. As they started down the driveway, Joshua glanced up. Staring at him from his aunt's front porch was Katie Higgins. She was wearing a soft, yellow dress trimmed in white lace. Her hair, no longer in tight braids, hung down her back in golden curls. Ice forgotten, Joshua stood and stared.

"Hi, Katie," was all he could manage. Suddenly, he was aware of how he must look. His shoes were dusty and scuffed, clothes wrinkled and covered in sweat. Quickly, he wiped his face with his sleeve, leaving a smudge of brown dirt on his nose. "We had to get ice," he tried to explain. It sounded a lame excuse for looking like a hobo at such a fine party.

"Come, Katie," called her mother.

Katie smiled and turned, following her mother inside. Joshua stood, a feeling creeping over him he could not identify. Soon, Mackie's impatient voice drove all thoughts of Katie from his mind. Thankfully,

Ramie heard Mackie's voice and came to help. Soon, the glacier size block was hoisted onto a table on the back porch. Sadie brought an ice pick from the kitchen, and handed it to Ramie, their hands touching. The boys watched as Ramie expertly cut the ice in small slivers, perfect for a punchbowl. Sadie put the ice in a pan, rinsed it, and put it in the ice box in the pantry. Each time she stepped back into the kitchen, Ramie's eyes followed. *He better watch where he's aiming that ice pick, instead of looking at Sadie,* decided Joshua. The boy thought for a moment. *I believe I got the same thing wrong with me that Ramie has. The symptoms are the same. Oh, my gosh! It must be catching!*

When there was enough ice cut for several parties, Sadie came back on the porch, her hands on her hips. "Get yourselves over to that hose and wash your faces and hands, and I'll fix you all a plate of goodies and punch fit for a king." Joshua reached the hose first, but was shoved aside by Mackie.

"You, too, Ramie," she ordered, her expression soft.

"Yes, Ma'am," he said, jumping up.

*He doesn't even look like himself with that silly expression on his face,* decided Joshua. As the cool water flowed over his hands, Joshua understood Ramie's strange behavior. "He's in love," the boy realized, mumbling to himself. "Ramie isn't sick, he's just acting strange. He's in love with Sadie, and it's making him act and talk silly." He remembered an old raccoon that came staggering in the yard one early spring. The police came and shot it, and later found out it had rabies. *I sure hope Ramie doesn't have rabies. He's my friend.*

"Are you going to stand there till the water wrinkles your fingers?' asked Mackie, impatiently. He came over and turned off the water. "Come on. There's a tray full of goodies on the porch, and I aim to dive in!"

Joshua hurried behind his friend, filled a plate with dainty sandwiches, fruit slices, nuts and mints. Glasses of fruit punch, filled with slivers of ice were waiting on a tray. Ramie, showing no interest in the food, whispered in Sadie's ear, causing her to smile and giggle. Mackie hovered around the table, eyes darting from one delicacy to another. Joshua, tired from the errand, sat down on the top step. Before he could take a drink of the icy liquid, he heard the screen door close. A moment later, Katie Higgins was smiling down at him.

"Hello, Joshua," she said softly, joining him on the top step. It didn't seem to bother her that she might get dirty. Up close, the dress reminded him of lemon custard with whipped cream.

"Do you want a cold drink?" he asked, his throat constricting.

"No thanks," she replied in a soft voice. He watched as wisps of long blonde hair move in the gentle breeze. Afraid she might see him staring he looked at his plate of dainty snacks. The tiny frosted cake he looked forward to eating, suddenly tasted like white glue the art teacher used in school. His mouth was too dry to even try a peanut or mint. Sliding his plate under a chair, he turned and stared in the big brown eyes of the girl beside him. "I need to check my grandfather's boat. Would you like to come with me?" He hoped his voice didn't sound too strained.

"Sure. I'll have to tell mama."

"I'll meet you out front," he said, anxious to get out of Mackie's range.

Joshua glanced at the girl walking beside him. It felt different from being with one of his friends. He slowed his pace. "How is your new baby?" he asked, breaking the awkward silence.

"It's just like you said, babies are a lot of work, and when you bring one home, your life is never the same again." Katie paused under the shade of a giant elm. "It's like getting a new puppy. Every day you love them a little more."

"Yeah, I can't imagine what it would be like if we never had Amy. At least now I don't have to be the *baby* of the family."

"Yeah, and I don't have to be an only child. People always think you're spoiled if you're an only child."

"Are you spoiled?"

"Of course."

The young couple paused on the edge of the breakwall and stared at the boats moored along the shore. Papa Tom's skiff rode peacefully at anchor. "Want to sit on the end of the dock?" asked Joshua.

"Sure," Katie replied.

After a long silence, Joshua said, "I have to go home tomorrow."

"I knew it would be soon."

"I'm sorry we didn't see more of each other this summer. I was working in Papa Tom's store almost every day."

"I was busy helping Mama with the baby."

"Next summer I'll take you for a ride in Papa's boat, and teach you how to row." Instantly, he was sorry he had spoken. The U.S. Fisheries Laboratory on Pivers Island had a fleet of row boats. Katie probably learned how to row when she was a toddler.

"That would be great."

"Do you know how to row a boat?" he asked cautiously.

Katie smiled. "I know a little, but," she hurried on, "I don't know where all the good fishing places are. My daddy is too busy to go exploring like you and your grandfather."

Joshua sat straighter, his chest swelled. "Wait for me, Katie. Next summer we'll explore every inch of the shore and marshlands. I'll take you fishing, and show you how to bait a hook."

A car horn interrupted.

"Oh, that's Mama. I have to go." Katie scrambled to her feet before Joshua could lend a hand.

"Katie," he called, "can I sit with you in church tomorrow?"

Katie stopped and glanced over her shoulder. "I would like that." She gave a final wave and disappeared inside the car.

Joshua stood on the end of the dock and looked across the channel at the distant island. "Oh, Lord, help me. My best friend threatens to beat me up at least once a day, and I think I'm in love with a wild girl who lives on a spooky island."

Joshua returned to the home on Moore Street in time to see Mackie and Ramie trying to outdo each other blowing smoke rings. Mackie turned to him. "Nobody's looking, sissy pants. Let's see if you can blow a smoke ring."

"No thanks. I haven't forgotten the look Clara gave me when she found out I had been smoking."

"You can go to church with me if you promise not to squirm or whisper, Sarah told her little sister. Nancy will be sitting with us, and she has no patience with little kids that talk in church, or anywhere."

"I promise, Sarah. I'll be good. I won't even take a deep breath, if you promise not to park me in the nursery." Sarah selected a pew near the front of the church so her little sister could watch the service. During communion, the gray haired priest, in his flowing vestments, placed his gentle hands on Amy's head and blessed her. During the lengthy sermon, Sarah's mind wandered back over the summer. She thought about her decision to be a school teacher, and remembered Miss Nettie saying teaching is a sacred trust. It's not only your responsibility to teach students their ABC's, but you must love them, even the unlovable, especially the unlovable.

From the corner of her eye, she watched her brother. He was sitting straight, keeping the place in his prayer book, and sitting as close to Katie Higgins as he dared. It seems like yesterday he begged to be allowed to come to church barefoot, and now he's sitting with his sweetheart. Sarah knew he liked Katie, since he had difficulty swallowing at the mention of her name.

After a dinner of fried chicken, mashed potatoes, butterbeans and sliced tomatoes, complete with apple cobbler, Sarah dragged her suitcase from the bottom of the closet. She packed the few clothes she had not moved to the bedroom upstairs, and took the suitcase up to Amy's room. As she was searching for clothes hidden under the bed or tucked away in the corner of a dresser drawer, Granny Jewel came and stood in the doorway.

"Girls, I have been thinking, and I believe my eldest granddaughter needs a room finer than the one off the kitchen. It seems a perfect room for a young man. I wouldn't be opposed to Frisky sleeping in there, as long as he kept his fleas out of the rest of the house.

"Joshua won't be too happy with pink walls, and a flowered bedspread."

"I can take care of that. This winter Mr. Fuller can paint the room a light blue, and I'll order a Lone Ranger bedspread and matching curtain." Granny Jewel crossed the room and sat on the edge of the bed. "I have to have a project, something to keep me busy during the long winter days," she said, her voice hollow. She looked around the room. "What color would you like?"

"I've outgrown pink. Maybe cream, with white trim."

"That sounds lovely, dear. New white shades and sheer white panels will give you privacy, and allow the cool breeze to pour in."

"All aboard! All aboard for Raleigh, and points west." Papa Tom, trying to sound cheerful, awakened the girls. Over on the next street, Mr. Peavy cleared his throat and attempted to awaken the rest of the town. "Put on the outfit I laid out for you, Amy, and I'll make up the bed. Papa Tom wants to get an early start, so we have to hurry."

At breakfast, Clara was making no attempt to hide her tears. She served the eggs and bacon while dabbing her eyes with the hem of her apron. "I'll clean up the kitchen, then I'm going home, 'cause I can't stand to listen to the silence."

"Come on, Sis," called Papa Tom. "Bring that suitcase down and let's shove off." He stood at the foot of the steps, looking lovingly at his oldest grandchild, now a young woman. *I won't cry,* he thought, *I won't cry.* "Clara packed enough food to last us three days. I hope I can find room for it."

Sarah rushed to the kitchen to give Clara one last hug. "You young'uns come back next summer, you hear? Those two old folks wait all year for June first."

"I promise, Clara. We'll be back before you know it." Sarah hurried through the house. Everyone was waiting in the car, the door on the driver's side still open. "Papa," she asked, looking in the window. What are you doing in the back seat?"

"Joshua, Frisky and I are waiting to be driven to Raleigh. You womenfolk sit up front."

Sarah hurried around the car and got in before her grandfather could change his mind. The smooth ivory of the large steering wheel felt wonderful to her touch. Turning the key, the powerful engine roared. Slowly, Sarah maneuvered the magnificent automobile out into the street, and headed west.

*I'll be back* she told the towering elms, their boughs meeting overhead. As the car glided smoothly across Beaufort bridge, Sarah glanced out of the window. *I'll be back,* she silently promised the sea gulls sitting on a fish house dock, waiting for someone to throw them a fish. Sarah's eyes misted. *I'll be back,* she promised. *I'll be back my eighteenth summer.*

If you enjoyed Seventeenth Summer . . .

Secrets, surprises and disappointments all crowd the pages of Eighteenth Summer.

Sarah's dear friend, Nancy must pick up the pieces of a dream shattered and go on with her life. With advice from Sarah she is able to do so.

Cousin Marnie must endure weeks hidden in a tiny room in her grandmother's home. The only person she will trust with her terrible secret is Sarah, the cousin whose feelings she has delighted in hurting every summer.

A tall stranger singles Sarah out from a group of friends at the Fourth of July parade. During their chance encounter Sarah once more receives a proposal of marriage.

Granny Jewel consoles a dear friend it is believed is suffering from a fatal illness. However, her friend with eyes sparkling and laughter in her voice, relieves Granny Jewel's worse fears.

Sarah receives a letter from Ohio and can hardly wait to know its contents. She is heartbroken to learn her friend of six years is in love. Words in the letter like, 'special' and 'friend' do nothing to mend a wound in her young heart.